ALEX WAGNER

ONLY MURDERS IN THE FOREST

A Case for the Master Sleuths

1

My paws flew over the forest floor as if I were weightless and could run like this forever. This was how it felt to be completely in your element! As I pulled along and ran, ran and ran, I could have howled wildly with joy.

The wind whistled around my ears, the forest floor was hard and cool, and behind me I could hear the delighted cries of my passengers, who were cheering me on to an even more daring pace. I stepped it up a notch and soared into seventh sled-dog heaven.

For the first time in my life, I was being allowed to pull a sledge. Well, it was only a very small vehicle, not one of those huge sledges against which my ancestors in Alaska had once demonstrated their incredible strength. And it had wheels instead of runners, because there wasn't much snow in our Tyrolean vacation destination at this time of year—apart from the ski slopes, which were of course covered in artificial snow for the tourists. But as passionately as I love snow in general, I didn't care at this moment that I was racing along a bare forest path, with leaves and earth under my paws instead of the wonderfully cool white splendor of winter.

My human, Victoria, and my feline friend, Pearl—both of whom being real lightweights—were sitting in the little wagon I was pulling, and I hardly noticed the load. Pearl squealed with delight, even though she was normally an inveterate sofa cat and wanted absolutely nothing to do with wind and cold. She was clearly enjoying the wild ride through the wintry forest, despite having crawled into Victoria's warm anorak with only her pink snub nose visible, sticking out of it.

"Faster, Athos!" she meowed, while Victoria hooted like a child on a rollercoaster.

What a success!

I could have gone on like this forever, but when Victoria finally decided we should make our way back to our hotel, I suddenly realized that we were no longer alone in the forest.

The unmistakable smell of my fellow canines caught my nose, and at the same time I heard excited barking. I counted three—no, four—dogs from the different voices, and the next moment I spotted two of them.

"Police dogs?" I heard Pearl's voice piping up behind me.

Two German shepherds appeared in front of us, snuffling between the tree trunks, each of them dragging a uniformed officer behind them on a lead. The dogs were panting wildly, casting about left and right, but couldn't seem to find a scent.

"Hey!" I shouted. "What are you looking for?"

Excitedly, I turned off the path to run towards one of the German shepherds—forgetting that I was harnessed to a sled.

Victoria's startled scream brought me to a halt just in

time, not a dog's length before I would have run between two tree trunks, which would have given the wagon behind me a very nasty beating. *I* would have easily fit between the trunks, but my vehicle was much wider than me.

I was startled. I'd almost put my passengers in danger! As a sled dog, I still had a lot to learn.

But the detective in me couldn't contain his curiosity. What were these police dogs and their two-leggeds doing here in the forest?

I barked wildly and managed to attract the attention of both the K9 nearby and his human. The German shepherd seemed very serious and conscientious, and utterly focused on his task. He would probably have ignored me and continued to search the forest floor with complete concentration if his human hadn't stopped and approached us.

The policeman, a short, pot-bellied but very strong-looking human, greeted Victoria politely. At first he stared at her with a deadpan expression, but when he saw Pearl a smile flitted across his face.

"Well, isn't she cute!" he commented—a reaction that I must have seen hundreds of times by now, but which Pearl could never get enough of.

She meowed like the most adorable of little kittens, to the policeman's ears, while in reality she was addressing the police dog: "Are you looking for a body here in the forest?"

"Pearl!" I hissed. "Don't always be so morbid!"

The K9 opened his snout and panted in surprise—a reaction that was not unfamiliar to me either. He probably saw Pearl as a harmless and ultra-cute little piece of fluff, and neither her fearless way of approaching him nor her blunt question about a corpse fitted that picture.

However, my cat friend seemed once again to have hit the mark dead-on.

"Two possible corpses," the police dog replied, after recovering from his astonishment. "But they might still be alive after all ... or at least my two-legged hopes so."

He threw out his chest. "We're the best search team around, but neither I nor my colleagues have found anything yet. The two women seem to have disappeared several days ago and people don't even know if we're looking in the right place here in the forest. To top it all it's been raining cats and dogs, and even the best nose has its limits."

He grumbled in frustration. "Can you perhaps help us? Are you from around here? Did you see or smell anything?"

"No, I'm sorry, we're just tourists," I replied reflexively.

As wildly and happily as I had been galloping through the forest for the last half hour, I would certainly have missed every scent trail, even if it had been a virtual scent highway. But of course I kept that to myself; after all, I didn't want to look like a complete amateur to the K9.

He was a most imposing animal. Quite a bit older

than me, experienced and fearless and, above all, thoroughly athletic. I suddenly felt rather plump next to him and, against my will, I had to think of those so-called fitness clubs where the two-leggeds like to torture themselves to get a sporty figure. I wondered if there might be such a thing for dogs? I had never heard of one, but if there were treadmills for humans, why not something for the likes of me? I would certainly have enjoyed the workout, and I would soon have become just as muscular as this search and rescue K9.

"Have you looked around the forest for possible witnesses?" Pearl addressed the German shepherd again. "Someone must have seen something."

"Witnesses?" the dog repeated.

The tiny one gave me a sideways glance, which was probably meant to express something like: *Is he slow on the uptake or what?*

"Well, the animals that live here in the forest," she explained to the police dog. "There must be a number of them. And someone will have always observed something, at least in our experience."

"In your experience?"

Dear me, is he a parrot or what? I read from Pearl's miniature snout.

"Of course," she said aloud. "My dog and I have already solved several murders."

The K9 looked impressed. "*Your* dog? And you're questioning witnesses? That's not what we're trained for. Our humans do that, they interrogate witnesses—

and suspects of course—but naturally they only question other two-leggeds."

"That's usually pointless. The two-leggeds hardly ever notice anything," said Pearl. "They can't hear or see very well and they can't smell worth a damn. And the murderers are usually smart enough to stay away from other people when they want to kill someone. Or if there are witnesses, they bump them off afterwards."

The K9's muzzle remained wide open.

His human exchanged a few words with Victoria, but my fellow canine soon urged him to get back to work—not just out of a sense of duty, I thought, but mainly to cover up his own confusion.

He pressed his nose to the ground, pulled on the leash and finally dragged his human partner away. It seemed that he wasn't ready to give up just yet.

If there were indeed dead bodies in this forest, he would certainly find them, I thought to myself. He and his K9 colleagues, who were now only making themselves heard through occasional distant barking. They would be successful even without interrogating witnesses, thanks to their highly trained noses alone.

Pearl peered curiously into the dense forest. She would certainly have liked to go looking for the missing two-leggeds herself, but she would have inevitably gotten her fur dirty, which slowed her thirst for action a little.

"Luckily it's not up to us this time," I said to her. "The police have to solve this case themselves—if it's a murder case at all."

The sniffer dog had not elaborated on why the two two-leggeds he was looking for were missing, but he had at least hinted that they might still be alive. I hoped so, even though I didn't know the two women.

Pearl gave me a pitying look. "Of course it's a murder case," she told me. "And we *are* going to solve it. That's obvious. Or are you going to leave it to these amateurs who don't even know how to find witnesses?"

2

When we returned to our hotel with Victoria shortly afterwards, I suspected that the tiny one might be right once again. Unfortunately, Pearl almost always is—at least as far as murder cases are concerned.

In the lobby of our rustic hotel, a large building made of stone and wood, we met Tim, our other two-legged and Victoria's boyfriend. And what was he doing? He was talking about murder! My heart dropped into my hind paws.

Tim was still in his wheelchair, because he had recently suffered serious injuries during one of our murder cases, and he was engaged in a lively conversation with a young man he called Henrik.

By contrast, the hotel lobby seemed so cozy and peaceful. The floor was laid of dark wooden planks polished with a pleasantly scented wax. In the corner opposite reception stood a tiled stove which, as a keen student of human history, I estimated to be over a hundred years old—and staring down at us from the walls were the skulls and antlers of countless dead deer, and that, now that there was talk of murder, perhaps did seem a little eerie.

Tim rolled towards us and immediately introduced Victoria to the person he'd been talking to. "This is Henrik Engel, darling. Imagine, he's a die-hard true crime fan, so he investigates murder cases ... um, a lot like us."

"Except we're not *fans* of it," Victoria mumbled, but so quietly that I'm sure only Pearl and I heard her words.

Henrik took Victoria's hand and shook it. He was quite a muscular guy—he must have been a regular at one of those gyms I mentioned earlier. He had a bulbous nose, rather fleshy lips, but friendly brown eyes that made his face somehow attractive.

"My wife and my sister-in-law founded our investigative team," he explained to Victoria. "You may have heard of them: the *Crime Sisters*. A few articles have been written about them and they've been on the radio."

"No, sorry," said Victoria. "Tim and I purposely don't deal with murder in our spare time. We, um, always stumble into our cases somehow, you know."

"The murders practically follow us around," Tim added glumly.

Henrik nodded, even though he looked rather astonished at the same time.

"Well, it doesn't matter if you don't know about us," he said. "Natalia, Fabienne and I—we're a great team, even if I only joined much later. But now it seems they've disappeared, and I'm terribly worried!"

He suddenly looked far less self-confident, indeed like the picture of misery.

"So the search and rescue dogs are out in the forest

because of them?" Victoria speculated. "That's terrible. What exactly happened?"

"I wish I knew." Henrik grimaced. "We came here to the hotel two weeks ago, probably for the same reason as you two, I suppose—to explore the Killer's Wood, from which so many have never returned. Natalia called it the Forest of Shadows ... she has a flair for the dramatic, you know, albeit in a positive way. She knows how to spin a breathtaking story out of almost any incident. People can listen to her for hours when she tells them about a series of murders."

"Wait," Tim interrupted the man. "The *Killer's Wood*? People who haven't returned? What's that supposed to mean?"

Henrik's brown eyes widened. "Don't tell me you haven't heard anything about it. You're amateur detectives, aren't you? You told me that you've solved several murders."

"That's correct," Tim said, "but as Victoria indicated, we're not actively looking for cases."

"Then you're not here at the hotel to solve the riddle of the Killer's Wood?" asked Henrik.

Victoria replied in the negative, and with an unhappy expression. "We just wanted to go on vacation and relax without any corpses for a change."

"Unbelievable," Henrik muttered, but then he immediately went on to tell us more about the eerie woodland we had ended up vacationing in the midst of—all unaware.

"There are many forests like this all over the world," he said. "Lonely areas where people keep disappearing ... or where people deliberately go to take their own lives. In Japan, for example, we visited such a forest once. An experience I will remember for the rest of my life! And don't forget the USA—some of the national parks in America seem to be cursed. Natalia said that it's not just possible serial killers going around, but that there must be other forces behind it. Dark forces, you see, that go far beyond mere human cruelty. Natalia longed to investigate on site, but we hadn't yet saved up the necessary capital."

"Your wife seems really adventurous," said Tim.

"My wife? No, no, Natalia is my sister-in-law. Fabienne is my wife."

"Oh, sorry, my mistake," Tim said. Was he thinking the same thing as I? That Henrik had spoken to us so enthusiastically about Natalia, but hadn't said a single word about Fabienne...?

He didn't mention her now, either. Instead, he continued to tell us about other forests with dark reputations. His descriptions made me feel quite queasy, but Tiny meanwhile sat upright, her ears pricked up, seeming to be enjoying the scary stories very much.

I thought he was never going to finish, but Victoria finally managed to interrupt his endless flow of words and asked him a question instead.

"When exactly did your wife and sister-in-law disappear?" she wanted to know.

"It will be a week tomorrow," Henrik said. He pinched his lips together.

"And the police are only now using search and rescue dogs?" asked Victoria.

Henrik suddenly looked embarrassed. "I didn't call the police straight away, you see. At first, I thought that Natalia and Fabienne—well, that they'd just left. My wife and I had an argument, and that happens from time to time. It's the way it is in most marriages, isn't it? At first, I wasn't worried that anything serious might have happened to them. And when I returned to our hotel room on the evening of the same day, their luggage was missing, so I just assumed that they had gone home. Without me, you understand? I waited here for a few more days, hoping that Fabienne would calm down and come back to me—but she didn't. I tried to contact her by phone, but when I couldn't manage that either, I left too. But when I reached home, there was only an empty apartment waiting for me. I went to Natalia's, of course, but they weren't there either."

He exhaled a soft groan. "I waited a few more days, but in the end I started to really worry. Fabienne can be resentful, but just disappearing off the face of the earth ... that's really not like her. So I went to the police station and reported her missing, along with Natalia, who hadn't turned up either. And now I've come back here to look for them both."

"Could it be that the two of them had to go into hiding?" asked Tim. "Maybe because they found out something explosive about your current investigations here in the Killer's Wood?"

Henrik frowned. "But then they could at least have called me!"

He ran both hands through his hair. "Oh God, if only nothing dreadful has happened to them! I hope the police dogs can find their trail after all this time."

3

We returned to our hotel suite. It was a large, bright room with plenty of wood and woolen fabrics and a ground-level patio from which you could walk directly into the forest. I had already used this exit the previous night, right after our arrival.

The hotel that Tim and Victoria had chosen for our vacation was located in the Tyrolean Alps, surrounded by peaks and gorges, alpine meadows, waterfalls and forests and many, many ski slopes. It was called *Alpenrose*, alpine rose, although at the end of January there was of course no sign of the flowers that gave the hotel its name.

Victoria flopped onto the sofa that was positioned next to the large double bed and groaned. "What's wrong with us, Tim? Of all the possible hotels in the Alps, why did we have to choose this one, which is apparently in the middle of a *Killer's Wood*, and where two women have just gone missing? I mean, are we truly cursed, or how else are we supposed to explain this?"

"I really didn't know about this so-called Killer's Wood when I booked the hotel," Tim said. "I honestly didn't."

"That's not what I actually meant—you don't find out something like that on a hotel website or from any reviews on the booking page. I didn't mean to criticize you. I just can't believe that we are constantly confronted with murder cases at every turn, no matter where we go. And that's been the case for—"

She looked at Tim with a pained expression in her eyes.

"I don't know either ... since we met?" he hazarded.

"For quite a while," said Victoria. "I was involved in the first murder case before Pearl even came to me. Actually, it was her mistress who was killed—"

She lowered her head and ran both hands through her dark brown hair, which still reminded me of a rough-haired dachshund's coat, even if it was a little longer now and no longer stuck out in all directions. The hairstyle suited her, I thought, but what do I know about human ideals of beauty?

"We're not getting involved in this case this time, okay?" said Tim. "If anyone *was* murdered at all. Maybe the two missing women really have just left—maybe they both wanted to be rid of this Henrik."

"But he makes such a harmless impression," said Victoria.

"Which, as we know, unfortunately proves nothing," said Tim.

"Yes, that's so—but stop right there! We must not start speculating about him! We're already on the verge of slipping into this case the way we always do."

Tim grimaced. "You're right! So then, let's change the subject. How was your sleigh ride with Athos? How did he do as a draught animal?"

Victoria essayed a smile. "Great—we all had a blast. Even our plush little sofa tiger." She bent down and lifted Pearl to her on the couch. Her fingertips began to stroke Tiny's head.

"*Sofa tiger*? Pah, I'm all-terrain too," Pearl emphasized to me. "But who likes such nasty cold weather?"

"Um, how about me, for starters?" I dared to object.

But of course I was ignored.

"I can't wait to go sledging with Athos," Tim said cheerfully, "once my bones can take a bit of a shake."

He stared down at his arm and leg, which were both still in plaster casts. No doubt he longed for the future, when he would finally be able to walk on his own two feet again, instead of being forced to get around in a wheelchair.

"What's your plan for tomorrow?" he asked Victoria.

"I have my first cross-country skiing lesson scheduled for the morning. I'm really excited—wait, no! It's actually this afternoon."

She suddenly had her cell phone in her hand and seemed to be consulting her calendar. "I hope I don't break my neck," she added with a wry grin.

"While cross-country skiing?" asked Tim. "Rather unlikely. It's not a particularly dangerous sport."

"All the better," said Victoria.

"Oh, I envy you," Tim sighed. "I have to cram for this horrible exam, and I really have to do it at full speed if I don't want to fail. And I'm finally going to start looking for a new apartment—I'm going to browse the online listings."

He turned his head and looked Victoria straight in the eye. "Have you given any thought about moving in with me? Then I'll be able to look for something bigger." He smiled at her—full of joyous hope, it seemed to me.

Victoria returned his smile.

"I'd like to mostly live with you in Vienna," she said, "even if I don't want to give up my father's house entirely. And I need to finally start thinking about what I want to do in the future—professionally I mean. I must find a new job."

I was very pleased that she wanted to keep our house by the lake. I liked it very much, even though to be honest I'd actually preferred living on the North Sea island of Sylt, where we would probably only visit as tourists from now on.

"Job?" said Pearl. "What more does she want? She's already our—" Tiny broke off and seemed to be searching for the right word.

"Cat's paw? Detectives' henchwoman?" I offered. "Apparently she's not completely happy with that role."

"I don't understand why she's so squeamish," said Pearl. "We're having a lot of fun, aren't we?"

"You mean apart from the fact that we've almost been bumped off a few times? Or is that just part of the fun for you?"

Pearl wrinkled her pink snub nose. "As a top detective, you have to take a few small risks from time to time."

"*Small* risks? *From time to time*?"

"Oh, don't be such a wimp, Athos!"

"There's no hurry to find your new job," Tim said to Victoria. He scooted as close to her as possible and then deftly maneuvered himself out of his wheelchair and onto the sofa. She wrapped her arm around his shoulders.

"With all our inheritances, treasure trove finder's fees and other money that has fallen into our laps, you really don't even *have* to go to work," he said. "As far as that goes, we honestly can't complain. Maybe this windfall is some kind of—I don't know—compensation from Fate for having helped hunt down all those murderers?"

Victoria frowned, but at the same time she stroked Tim's arm gently.

"Didn't you want to do something like criminal psychology?" Tim asked. "Maybe go back to university ... or take a few courses?"

"I would be interested in the subject," said Victoria, "but somehow I'm also afraid that we might end up involved in in even more crime and murder than we already are."

"What's she moaning about?" said Pearl in her inimitably sensitive way. "Hunting murderers is an exciting sport! Much better than poring over boring history books and constantly living in the past, as Tim does with his studies. Or poking around in people's souls like Victoria did in her old job."

Our human snuggled closer to her boyfriend and seemed to have nothing else to say for the moment.

He stroked her hair with his uninjured hand. "Now let's treat ourselves to a nice vacation," he said. "We've really earned it."

Victoria sighed contentedly. At least they seemed to have managed to stop thinking about the Killer's Wood and the missing women.

Pearl, however, would never have dreamed of letting a few bodies slip through her paws.

"So it's up to us once again to solve these murders, Athos," she said in the tone of an experienced super sleuth. "How do you think we should best approach the investigation?"

"Couldn't we maybe just take a vacation, too?" I asked timidly. "We deserve a breather, I think."

She looked at me as if colorful mushrooms were suddenly growing on my head, and didn't even deign to comment on my suggestion.

Instead, she trudged towards the patio door and stared out into the forest that surrounded the hotel. "If two-leggeds vanish out there, we'll have to check out the area around the hotel for better or worse."

"Seriously?" I asked. "You want to leave this cozy room? *Voluntarily*? When it's so cold and inhospitable outside? And probably quite windy, too."

I peered up at the nearby treetops, which weren't moving at all. But hopefully Pearl wouldn't notice.

My attempt to dissuade her from her plan, and encourage her to simply spend a leisurely afternoon in the suite with our two-leggeds without chasing murderers, bounced off her fluffy façade. She was *determined*.

She scratched at the glass pane of the French window with her front paw and meowed loudly. Victoria turned her head and looked over at her.

"What is it, sweetie?" she asked.

Pearl repeated her maneuver. Scratching. Meowing.

Victoria smiled. "Really now? *You* want to go out? Into the cold?"

My words exactly—but unfortunately Pearl was persistent.

And so it was that Victoria finally got up and opened the patio door for the murder-hungry tiny one.

4

Of course I trotted out into the open right behind Pearl, even though my thirst for adventure was definitely limited. After all, someone had to protect this crazy little kitten as she plunged headlong into a madcap adventure once again. Otherwise, the leading international detective she thought herself to be might possibly fall victim to an attack within the first few meters of forest. Pearl was so small that she was a potential tasty morsel for all kinds of woodland predators. Martens, foxes, birds of prey....

So I trotted along behind her.

Of course, Pearl's plan to "look around outside" didn't mean that she was walking straight into the wilderness.

You didn't seriously believe that, old boy, I thought to myself, amused. No, Pearl walked alongside the building for the time being, content to sniff around and occasionally peek into the forest.

I refrained from pointing out that we certainly wouldn't find a killer here in the shadow of the hotel who was up to mischief out in the solitude of the woods.

What we finally found—or rather, who—was a woman smoking a cigarette on one of the other patios on this side of the hotel. She reacted with the usual enthusiasm at the sight of Pearl that my feline friend evoked in most people.

"Hey, you cute little thing," she exclaimed and came walking towards us as soon as she spotted us. She went down on her knees in front of Pearl and at least gave me a friendly look. In other words, she wasn't too scared of me, a reaction which unfortunately happened quite often when we met new people.

Pearl wrinkled her nose, but graciously allowed her a few caresses. She didn't like the smell of smoke emanating from the woman any more than I did.

Apart from that, the human seemed nice enough, and quite fond of animals. She was slim, looked very toned and athletic and had long, blond hair—the Labrador type—that fell almost to her hips. She was wearing a dirndl with a silk apron, a traditional dress that was often seen in this part of the country, and a woolen vest. Probably so she wouldn't freeze to death out here while she was smoking.

I peeked through the patio door that was half open behind her. The room beyond it was not a hotel suite like the one we were living in, but an office. Two large desks stood opposite each other, the walls covered by cupboards and shelves, and in one of the corners there was a monstrosity of the kind the two-leggeds used to print out all kinds of documents.

Just as I was looking into the office in question, a man entered the room. He was also dressed in traditional costume, which made him look somewhat like a hunter, but he probably actually wasn't one. I had already learned that here in the hotel, the employees were all required to wear traditional clothing, which probably appealed to the tourists.

At second glance, however, I realized that this human was not a simple employee—his name was Leonard Zauner and he was the boss and owner of the Hotel Alpenrose. He had greeted Victoria and Tim personally when we'd arrived, but was not an animal lover particularly. Pearl and I were welcome at the hotel, but we had been greeted with more enthusiasm elsewhere.

Anyway, Leonard Zauner glanced around the room, spotted the woman who was still stroking Pearl, and came straight towards us.

He stepped out onto the patio almost silently, smiled suddenly and then crept up behind the female two-legged. When he reached her, he whispered in a tender tone: "Hello darling, what are you doing?"

The woman was startled. She straightened up quickly and whirled around. When she saw who had stalked up behind her, however, she immediately relaxed again. What's more, her face literally began to glow.

"Oh it's you, my love," she replied in an equally tender tone and immediately wrapped her arms around the hotelier's neck.

He pulled her close and pressed a kiss to her temple. Only then did he notice Pearl and me, although we really couldn't be overlooked. I mean, sure, Pearl is small, but *I'm* really not a midget pinscher.

"These two belong to the new arrivals in room four," he explained to the woman, who was apparently his girlfriend.

But she already knew that: "Yes, Martha has told me about them. She had a hard time tidying the room this morning. This plump husky apparently sheds quite a bit."

The insult caught me unawares.

I mean, the fact that people thought I was an overweight husky when I was in fact a sturdy Malamute was something I had almost got used to by now, and comments to that effect bounced off me—off my thick coat that is, which I really appreciated, even if it perhaps made me look a bit bulky.

But *shedding hair*? *Me*? A little at most! And that was just as true for Pearl. But of course she was much smaller than me and therefore had less fur to shed. She also scored points with her cuteness factor again, so *her* hair went unmentioned. Really, it wasn't fair.

"The police are out again with the search dogs," Leonard told his girlfriend. He seemed a little older than her, but was also in good shape. His hair was of the poodle type—very curly and almost black, apart from the temples, which were already slightly graying. His traditional jacket was a bit tight around the shoulders, but I knew from experience that this was probably intentional—the two-legged women loved muscles on their men, and they often wore tighter clothes on purpose so that their own assets wouldn't be overlooked.

"Poor women," said the smoker, "if only they could be found—safe and sound!"

"That would be nothing short of a miracle," said Leonard. "Where would they have been all this time if nothing had happened to them?"

The woman shrugged her shoulders and seemed deeply worried.

He detached himself from her a little and looked her in the eye. "Sissi, you have to promise me you'll take good care of yourself, okay? I know how much you like wandering around in the woods, but I'm really worried, you know? I would never forgive myself if ... something happened to you."

She kissed him. "That's so sweet of you, darling, but I can't spend all my time hiding here in the house. I need the exercise, the fresh air, the forest. And why would this killer, if he even exists, choose me of all people?"

Leonard opened his mouth, but immediately closed it again. I had the impression that he'd wanted to say something important, but had then changed his mind.

Pearl distracted me. "Hmm, let's move on, Athos. This conversation really isn't all that revealing, after all. By the way, this Sissi is the chief housekeeper here at the hotel," she added. "I saw her this morning while you were still snoring. She's the boss of the maids who clean the establishment. And she seems to be very strict—her employees obey her every word."

"And apparently complain bitterly to her about our hair," I grumbled back.

"About *your* hair, Athos," Pearl replied promptly. And as if she wanted to let me know that her silky coat absolutely never fell out, she started a thorough grooming session. Apparently the continuation of our tour of exploration would have to wait a little longer.

5

Later we followed Victoria into the lobby of the hotel, where she was going to meet her instructor for cross-country skiing. Here we bumped into Henrik Engel again.

He was talking to an older man, who had a rather grumpy look on his face. I had the impression that Henrik must have been talking to him very forcefully for some time and was far from ready to give up on his demands.

When Henrik saw us—or rather, Victoria—something like new hope flickered in his eyes. "Oh, you see, Chief Inspector, here's the other true crime expert I mentioned. I'm sure she shares my opinion. Don't you, Victoria?"

Our human seemed taken by surprise—and quite rightly so, in my opinion.

"I beg your pardon?" she managed to say, looking intently at the door—presumably in the hope that her cross-country skiing instructor would turn up and get her out of this predicament.

However, her friendly and compassionate nature gained the upper hand, so she asked Henrik: "What's happened? Is it about your wife...?"

"Chief Inspector Weinhart wants to give up the search for Natalia and Fabienne. After only two days! The dogs can't possibly have already searched the entire forest."

"The *entire forest*?" the inspector roared. "Do you know what you're asking? We can only cover a certain radius around the hotel, and if the dogs can't pick up a scent here, we don't stand a chance. That's just the way it is. Investigations are not always crowned with success immediately, as you self-appointed super sleuths seem to imagine. And are putting yourself in danger if you're determined to cross paths with a murderer. That should have been clear to you and your partners from the start. I wish you and all the other enthusiastic true crime fans would leave the work to the professionals. The police force!"

"Who then do nothing, or throw in the towel straight away!" retorted Henrik.

The chief inspector groaned dramatically. He made a dismissive gesture with his hand, which was probably meant to indicate that he was fed up with this conversation and he didn't want to discuss the matter any further.

"Well, I'll keep looking myself!" Henrik exclaimed. "You can make fun of amateur detectives all you want, but unlike you, we are persistent. I'm not just going to ignore the fact that so many women have disappeared here in these damn woods. You know that as well as I do."

"Just because someone disappears doesn't mean we have to assume it's murder," the inspector countered. "We've been over this twice already. Accidents do happen in the mountains; there's nothing we can do about that. There's a lot of rough terrain around here, and an inexperienced hiker..."

"But my two girls didn't go hiking, for pity's sake!"

"Nevertheless, they could have had an accident. Or they simply *wanted to* disappear. You persist in ignoring this possibility too, my dear Mr. Engel. Wives leave their husbands every day, anywhere in the world. And perhaps your wife has just taken her sister with her—that is not unusual either. Need I remind you that you yourself were not sure where and when the two ladies actually disappeared?"

Henrik clenched his teeth, but said nothing more.

The chief inspector adopted a somewhat more conciliatory tone. "We will of course continue the investigation, but the search here on site is over for now. We'll stay in touch, Mr. Engel." He nodded politely to Victoria, then turned away and left the hotel.

Henrik suddenly grabbed onto Victoria's hand as if it were his lifeline. Only when he heard the surprised little sound she made did he let go of her, just as abruptly.

"Excuse me," he mumbled.

But then he looked into her face with the pleading eyes of a lost puppy. "Please, you have to help me. I'm sure Natalia hasn't just gone into hiding—and neither has Fabienne. They wouldn't leave me mad with worry for them like this. They're not that cruel."

"I—" Victoria began, but Henrik was already talking again. The words came faster and faster from his lips, as tears might have flowed from another two-legged.

"The people who've disappeared here in the forest over the years were all women, and they all stayed here at the Hotel Alpenrose—or worked here. Did you know that, Victoria? It really can't be a coincidence; you have to admit that! It's a sign that fate has brought you here. Such an experienced investigator. You must save Natalia and Fabienne—please!"

He took a step forward and came far too close to Victoria for comfort. I was just about to intervene with a warning growl when suddenly the front door of the hotel opened and a brightly smiling, really rather young man came breezing into the lobby.

He was very tall, had his light brown hair tied back in a ponytail and carried a small rucksack slung casually over his shoulder.

He looked around briefly, but then came straight towards us. "Victoria Adler?" he asked as he turned to my two-legged.

She nodded and I couldn't help but notice how relieved she was at his interruption.

"I'm Karl, your cross-country skiing instructor. We spoke on the phone. I'm very pleased to meet you." He shook her hand vigorously. "Are you ready to go?"

"Oh yes, that's me. All ready," Victoria said quickly.

Henrik's brow furrowed, giving him a gloomy, almost sinister look. But he said nothing more and made no attempt to keep Victoria back any longer.

Pearl and I trotted along behind our human, and I

was glad that I hadn't needed to intervene against Henrik. Despite his pushiness, I felt really sorry for him. It must be terrible to lose two members of your pack at once. I'm sure he blamed himself day and night for not protecting the two women well enough.

I yelped loudly to dispel these oppressive thoughts. Now I was really looking forward to a harmless adventure in the snow, and I hoped that Pearl's grumbling about the wintry weather would be limited.

6

Sometimes I find it really difficult to make sense of human behavior. I mean, if you're forced to go through life on only two legs—which must be a very wobbly affair in any case—why on earth would you strap miserably long, unwieldy boards under your feet to slide around on in the snow? And the two-leggeds don't see this as a punishment, but on the contrary as a particularly entertaining pastime! All too often, the humans' conversations are all about how many friends and relatives have had accidents or even died while skiing, and they carry on in spite of it.

To my great relief, cross-country skiing, the type that Victoria had chosen, seemed to be less dangerous than alpine skiing, which involved flying down steep mountain slopes at breakneck speed. Karl, the cross-country skiing instructor, led us to a trail that was very close to the hotel. It was beautifully covered with white snow and precise tracks, even though there was little else of such bright frosty splendor to be seen here in the valley.

Karl began to explain a few basic movements to Victoria, and of course Pearl and I did not stand idly by. We turned straight into the forest in the hope of finding some witnesses who might give us information about the whereabouts of the missing women. The police dogs hadn't used this source, and as always Pearl was convinced that we could do better.

However, the forest was not her natural element at all. She trudged along between withered leaves and puddles, and through swathes of mud, like a ballet dancer who didn't want to get her pretty white shoes dirty.

We had barely moved a short distance away from the two-leggeds when we heard Karl's voice behind us: "Your animals are running off into the woods, Victoria! Wouldn't you rather put them safely on a lead and tie them up somewhere?"

I couldn't see Victoria; we were already too far away for that, but I imagined she was smiling as she answered. "Oh, Athos and Pearl are very independent and like to roam about alone. Maybe they want to continue sniffing around where the professionals have failed."

"Excuse me?" Karl asked, obviously confused.

"I mean the police search and rescue dogs that were here in the forest today looking for the missing women. I can't imagine that Athos and Pearl will succeed where those trained sniffer dogs have failed, but who knows? The two of them always manage to surprise me."

She sounded kind of adventurous, I thought. Apparently, she had temporarily forgotten that she didn't want to investigate another murder case on her peaceful vacation.

"Pah," Pearl commented drily. "*We're* the real professionals, not those K9 dogs who wouldn't even think of looking for potential witnesses." Once again, she threw herself into a queen tiger pose and walked on with her head held high.

I could still hear the answer Karl gave Victoria, even though we were now some distance away from them: "But your kitten is still so small and helpless. I'd be terrified that something might happen to her."

Karl seemed like such a nice man. Someone who also cared about animals, not just his cross-country skiing students.

"Pearl is no longer a kitten, she's already fully grown," Victoria replied. "She just has a genetic peculiarity that means she'll always look like a kitten, but fortunately, it doesn't affect her health."

Karl was probably taken aback, because he didn't have an answer.

Very quietly, I heard Victoria's words: "Athos also takes very good care of the little one. He's the perfect bodyguard, you know."

I gave Tiny a meaningful look. *There you hear it!*

"But I don't need a bodyguard," came the decidedly ungrateful reply.

"What else then? A valet, perhaps?" I grumbled.

At least that amused her.

"A friend is quite enough for me, Athos," she said to my great astonishment—and I was happy with that. Of course, I still kept an eye out for possible predators that could be a danger to Tiny.

Here near the trail, however, we didn't see a single forest dweller, neither a predator nor any of our more harmless contemporaries.

"We need to get further away from the humans," I said to Pearl, and she responded with an ill-tempered grunt. I looked down at her paws and noticed that they were already quite dirty.

Poor little sofa cat. But as we all know, she would have put up with almost anything to preserve her image as a top-flight detective.

Unfortunately, as we walked on, I came to the realization that I was probably just as much of a deterrent to the shy animals of the forest as the humans were, what with my size and impressive set of teeth. Pearl even suggested that she would like to look around on her own, but of course that was out of the question—not here in the middle of the wilderness. She might think she didn't need a guardian, but I knew better.

"We'll find a witness," I said. "We've always managed to do that, haven't we? Just be patient."

Suddenly, without the slightest warning, a forest dweller did appear in front of us. I hadn't smelled him or heard the slightest telltale sound. He was lurking half hidden in the undergrowth, with only his large round eyes staring at us and his fur shimmering between the branches and twigs. He was light brown, but decorated with black spots.

Pearl let out a startled squeak, instinctively pressing herself against me. *She doesn't need a bodyguard, my foot.*

However, I was so surprised by the appearance of the mysterious forest dweller that not even a single snide remark crossed my lips.

The creature seemed to be almost as big as me, at least judging by its outline, which I tried to make out in the gloom.

I gathered up my courage.

"Hello," I barked, more fearlessly than I felt. "I'm Athos, and this is Pearl. Do you live here in the forest?"

This question didn't make much sense, because we certainly didn't have someone's pet standing in front of us. But what kind of creature could it be, that was approaching us so shyly?

"Show yourself," I encouraged the phantom. "We're definitely not going to hurt you."

"I am really not at all concerned about that," said a dark voice. It sounded velvety soft and very dangerous at the same time.

7

Beside me, Pearl's eyes widened as the forest dweller finally emerged from his hiding place—and I let out a startled yelp.

We had a big cat in front of us, the likes of which I had never seen in the flesh. A cat that was actually as big as me. His coat was very thick and fluffy, and covered all over with black spots. The tip of his tail was completely black, but the most unusual thing about him was his ears: thick dark hair grew at the tips, as if he were a painter who always carried two brushes with him.

"A lynx!" Pearl exclaimed. "Oh wow."

Now that she realized that she had a fellow cat—albeit a very large one—in front of her, she lost all trepidation. She toddled curiously towards the lynx and greeted him like a long-lost friend.

I jumped forward to stop her. Was she out of her mind? Cat or no cat, this lynx was a dangerous predator that could easily eat a half portion of feline like Pearl as a midday snack.

The lynx hissed; he probably thought I was threatening him.

Pearl turned to stare at me in amazement. She didn't seem to understand why I was so upset. "Don't worry, Athos," she said to me, in all seriousness!

Then she explained to the lynx: "We've come to you as

friends. We are four-pawed detectives looking for two missing women. Have you seen or heard anything that might help us?"

She tiptoed even closer to the lynx. Utterly tired of living! But luckily he only looked astonished, and not necessarily hungry.

"Hmm, you smell good," Pearl said after sniffing him, "and you're *sooo big*. Even bigger than Athos!"

"He's not," I heard myself protesting, but Pearl didn't seem to notice. She put her head back and stared almost reverently up at the lynx.

He eyed her curiously from above. "Are you trembling, little cat?" he asked. His tone suddenly sounded quite gentle and caring.

"Pearl is probably a bit cold. She's not much of an outdoor cat," I replied, before she could answer for herself.

A mistake—I earned a critical look from Tiny. She quickly said to the lynx: "What? No, not me! I'm a descendant of the great forest cats of the North. I have thick fur and am quite, er, agile off-road!"

I couldn't believe my ears.

The lynx was now sniffing at Pearl. He only stared at me from a distance with his big round eyes, the color of which reminded me of the amber that the humans so loved to collect.

I sat down demonstratively on my backside to signal to him that I wouldn't try to hurt him. As long as he left Pearl alone.

"You said you were detectives?" he asked Tiny. "Looking for two-leggeds? That's so ... unusual. I've never met any actual detectives before, apart from police dogs like the ones that came through my territory yesterday and today."

"We cats are much better sleuths than any police dog," said Pearl, spritely and confident as ever. "I've already solved plenty of murders—with the help of Athos," she added graciously. "And with our two-leggeds' aid as well, who act as our assistants."

"Remarkable," said the lynx.

Pearl sniffed him again—I could see it clearly. And she had such an entranced and delighted look on her face, as if she had just been served a festival-sized portion of freshly caught pink salmon.

"Have you seen the two women we're looking for, here in the forest?" she continued to question the big cat. "I'm afraid I don't know anything more specific about them—what they look like or anything—but apparently quite a few two-legged females have gone missing here in your territory before. A serial killer could be behind it, I think. You must have noticed him, right?"

"I generally avoid humans," said the lynx wryly. "But if you want, I'll ask around a bit."

"Oh yes, that would be great," chimed Pearl, in the sweetest most kittenish tone. And then she purred, too. I couldn't believe it!

"Okay," said the lynx. "Then wait here for a moment. I'll be right back."

He disappeared into the undergrowth.

Pearl blinked as if waking from a dream.

"What a cat," I heard her murmur. "Did you see his ears, Athos?" She turned her head dreamily towards me.

"What about them?" I grumbled. I was suddenly in a dreadful mood without being able to say why.

"They're so ... elegant, don't you think?"

"If you say so."

Pearl didn't complain once while we stood around in the cold waiting for the lynx to finally return.

"Would you like me to warm you up a bit?" I offered, but she declined with thanks.

"I have a nice thick coat myself," she explained.

The spotted feline returned to us just as abruptly as he had appeared the first time. The treetops above our heads were swallowing up the already sparse light of the winter afternoon, so that the lynx materialized before us like a shadow from the twilight. Once again, he had approached us from downwind, so we hadn't noticed him until he was right in front of us.

"No one here in the immediate vicinity has anything unusual to report," he said.

"Who did you ask?" I wanted to know. "Do many of your own kind live around here? Do you have a large pack?"

"Cats don't live in packs," Pearl lectured me.

I knew that, of course—in principle.

I felt a little stupid. But the idea of spending my whole life wandering around alone, without any friends and family by my side ... no, I didn't even want to try to imagine that.

The lynx seemed to notice what was going on inside my head. "I occasionally come across members of my own species," he said. "But only a very few of us live here in these woods."

"Then you must have many other friends, surely?" I asked. I was positive all kinds of animals called this area home.

The big cat's black brushy ears twitched. I couldn't help noticing how fascinated Pearl was with them.

"Most other animals fear me," said the lynx. "It's the trees of the forest that are my dearest companions."

"You can talk to trees?" I asked incredulously.

What would he come out with next? Was this proud tom about to unfurl a pair of wings and take to the skies? Pearl certainly would have squealed with delight.

"Trees can't talk, dog," the lynx explained to me. His words didn't sound condescending, but came across as very calm and relaxed.

"That is, they can amongst themselves, of course," he corrected himself, "but not with us animals. Just like we can't make ourselves understood by the humans. Unless you've lived with them for a very long time —with the trees, I mean. Then you understand them a bit, and you can become their friend. I look after the trees here in my forest, and they look after me. They warn each other of danger, support each other with food, fend off enemies, and make connections via their roots. And they are not afraid of me, like so many of the animals that live here."

"Then I guess we can't use the trees as witnesses." Pearl looked a little disappointed.

"Not so fast, little cat," said the lynx, amused.

"I'm not *that* small!" the tiny one exclaimed. She hated nothing more than someone commenting on her size.

The lynx still seemed amused, but continued in a serious tone: "I can sense when the trees perceive danger or violence, which would certainly have happened if a two-legged had killed another in the immediate vicinity. I have heard trees in other parts of my territory whispering of hatred and violence among the humans, but that has never interested me that much. The two-leggeds really aren't my favorite creatures."

"Hatred and violence?" I said to Pearl. "That doesn't sound like accidents or suicide to me—so maybe someone really has done something to all the women who are supposed to have disappeared in this forest."

"Definitely," said Pearl. "Otherwise it wouldn't be a new murder case for us, would it?"

"And of course we assume straight away that no matter where we go, there will always be one waiting for us," I grumbled.

"Exactly. That's just how it is, right?"

Unfortunately, I couldn't contradict her.

"If you would like me to, little cat, I'll walk my territory and ask around to see if people are really being murdered here in the forest," said the lynx.

"My name is Pearl," replied the tiny one.

"Oh yes, I'm sorry—where are my manners? As I said, I don't meet other cats very often."

He lifted his head and looked over at me. "Or dogs."

"We'll wait here, okay?" said Pearl. "Until you come back from your tour of your territory."

The fluffy ears of the big cat twitched again, and he was visibly amused this time. "My territory is very large, Pearl. It will be far longer before I can return to you."

"So much forest," murmured Pearl. Maybe she was just thinking it; I already knew her so well that I sometimes perceived thoughts of hers that were not meant for the ears of others.

The lynx turned to leave, but before he could completely disappear into the twilight of the undergrowth, Pearl called out: "Wait—what's your name?"

He stopped and turned to us. "No one has asked me my name in a very long time," he mumbled.

And that's what happens when you only have trees as friends but no pack to call your own, I thought to myself. I felt really sorry for the lynx. Wasn't he terribly lonely here in this seemingly endless forest?

"What did your mother call you?" I asked him. "And your siblings?"

He suddenly stood stock-still, bowed his head and seemed to lose himself in memories. A gentle, perhaps even slightly wistful expression came over his face.

"Moonshadow," he whispered. "That's what they called me. My mother and my brother, who I unfortunately lost after just a few weeks." His words were no more than a breath.

The next moment he had vanished into thin air, as silent as a phantom. Only a few branches shook where he had just been standing.

What a fitting name, I said to myself.

Pearl called after the lynx: "Don't you want to get to know our two-legged? Victoria, I'm sure she'd be thrilled to see you."

"I never show myself to a two-legged," came his reply, already from a surprisingly far distance away. "If word got out that I live here, they'd come into my forest and hunt me down."

"Surely that's forbidden now," I objected.

"And you think that will stop the humans?"

Those were his last words. The echo of his voice was lost in the soughing of the wind.

I had to give Pearl a gentle poke with my nose to bring her out of her reverie.

"Come on, let's go back to Victoria," I said. "She might be missing us already." I couldn't have told you how much time had passed since we'd met the lynx.

"What a hunk," muttered Pearl.

On the way back, she never once complained about

the mud or cold. She even trudged through the odd puddle without seeming to notice, and when I asked her if there was indeed something nasty going on in the forest, I got nothing more than a, "Mmmm, looks like it."

8

Victoria and Tim ended their evening in the small hotel bar downstairs, which was directly adjacent to the Alpenrose restaurant. During the day, cakes, pastries and coffee were served to a bustling clientele here, and now in the evening there were colorful cocktails and other sorts of alcoholic drinks that the two-leggeds loved to indulge in.

Like the rest of the building, both establishments were decorated with plenty of stone and wood, and the bar also had an open fireplace, which spread an unbearable warmth but also radiated a sense of coziness in the atmosphere. There were wide bookshelves on two of the walls, which exuded a pleasant bookish aroma and were well-stocked. Although I couldn't read, I always felt somehow at ease in the company of books.

Our two-leggeds seemed to be serious about keeping their vacation murder-free, because neither at dinner nor now in the bar did they mention so much as a word about the two missing women, or about the Killer's Wood in general, which we had so unwittingly chosen for our vacation.

Victoria talked about cross-country skiing, and Tim moaned about the enormous amount of material he needed to learn for his upcoming university exam.

The tiny one had behaved very strangely at dinner. The hotel was so pet-friendly that we were allowed into the restaurant—by no means a matter of course in such establishments—and Pearl and I had been served chicken in a delicious sauce.

Pearl, normally something of a glutton, had left half the portion, although she had initially had fulsome words of praise for the chef and his cooking after her first inspection of the dish.

I really hadn't experienced anything like it very often in all our time together.

Now, since we had followed our two-leggeds into the bar, Pearl was sitting upright like one of the statues of her beloved cat goddess by the large patio doors of the pub, staring out into the night. She couldn't have seen anything out there, even with her sharp eyes, because the lights in the room were mostly dimmed, but Pearl had taken up position right next to a large floor lamp whose reflection made the blackness of the night beyond the panes of glass seem absolutely impenetrable.

After listening to Tim and Victoria talk for a while, I started to get bored. A murder-free vacation was all well and good, but I realized that I was longing for a challenge, something to sink my teeth into. And I couldn't get the two missing two-leggeds out of my head, either: Natalia and Fabienne. What if they could still be rescued, and their fate lay in our paws?

I trotted over to Pearl and gave her a gentle nudge with my muzzle.

"Shall we continue working on our new case for a while?" I suggested. "Over there, in the armchair in front of the fireplace, is Henrik Engel. He looks terribly sad and he's getting drunk."

Pearl turned her head. "But there's no human with him whom he could talk to. We're unlikely to overhear anything new from him."

"The two-leggeds like talking to us too, don't they?" I countered. "Even if they think we don't understand a word they say. Maybe he'll want to pour his heart out to us."

"All right," said Pearl. "It can't do us any harm." Her words didn't sound at all enthusiastic, but she got up anyway and we trotted over to Henrik.

In his left hand he was holding a glass containing some gold-colored and very foul-smelling alcohol, and in his right was his cell phone, the screen of which he was staring at as if spellbound.

My height proved to be an advantage here, because I didn't have to climb onto his lap to find out what he was looking at. He was staring at a photograph of a pretty young woman with silver-blonde hair that was cut short, giving her a kind of cheeky look. She also had a snub nose that she very pertly stuck out. A two-legged woman who was very self-confident, it seemed to me, and who knew what she wanted.

I assumed that she was Henrik's wife Fabienne, whom he must have been worried sick about by now.

As if to confirm my thoughts, a single tear rolled down Henrik's cheek the next moment.

"The poor man is heartbroken," I said at once to Pearl. "Either his wife has left him or something bad has happened to her. We have to comfort him."

I immediately went into action, putting my snout on his thigh and wagging my tail encouragingly.

"Heartbreak?" Pearl repeated, suddenly seeming a little less absent-minded. "That's terrible."

She made a big leap and landed in Henrik's lap. At first she tried to glance at the photo he was looking at. He had swiped the display in the meantime, but the new picture showed the same woman. Again, she was grinning confidently, almost defiantly, into the camera.

"Pretty two-legged," was Pearl's verdict. Then she finally turned her attention to Henrik and began to purr sweetly.

Whereupon another tear rolled down Henrik's cheek. As if in slow motion, his lips formed a kiss, which he blew to the beauty in the photo.

"Oh, my darling," he whispered wistfully. "My one and only. Where are you—are you all right?"

Then he swiped the display again, and this time a video began to play. The silver-blonde woman was also in it, but this time an equally attractive, slightly shorter woman with darker and much longer hair was sitting at her side.

The next moment, this woman said to the silver-blonde: "You're really awful, Natalia!" She poked her playfully, then ran her hand tenderly through her hair and finally gave her a kiss on the cheek.

The audio was very quiet, but loud enough for dog or cat ears, and the video ended at this point. It was probably just a brief snapshot that had been taken spontaneously.

Henrik switched off his cell phone. He placed it on the armrest of his chair and began to stroke Pearl with his free hand.

"*Natalia?*" I repeated, puzzled. "But then..."

"...is the silver blonde he misses so much not his wife?" Pearl asked.

"But his sister-in-law?"

Pearl wrinkled her nose. "That's not nice at all. He should miss his wife—Fabienne."

She jumped off Henrik's lap and joined me on the floor. There she started a grooming session, even though her coat was sparkling clean. Victoria had put us both in the bathtub after our trip into the forest, because we'd admittedly returned to her covered in mud.

Henrik stared down at Pearl, probably feeling let down because she had withdrawn from his caresses. His eyes moistened again, but then he suddenly jumped up and hurried towards the exit of the bar, swearing quietly to himself.

We did not follow him.

Instead, we walked to the counter, where a lively conversation was going on between two of the hotel employees. They were both women, and I wondered what they were talking about so intently.

One of them was standing behind the bar, the other sitting in front of the counter on one of the high stools. Apart from that, there were no other two-leggeds nearby.

I recognized the seated woman as Sissi, the chief housekeeper who had flirted so lovingly with the hotel's owner that afternoon. She was dressed up like a star actress, in eye-catching make-up and a silky, shimmering, floor-length green dress. She was wearing the kind of high-heeled shoes that would inevitably break your ankles, although amazingly the two-legged ladies always managed to keep their balance somehow.

We learned from their conversation that the barmaid's name was Tracy. She was younger than Sissi and was wearing a rather inconspicuous traditional outfit. Her hair was dark, and she had almost black eyes and a rather flat nose. Not quite like a bulldog, mind you, but still quite flat.

Their conversation revolved around a man called Alessio, with whom Tracy was apparently hopelessly in love. I got the impression that he also worked at the hotel somewhere, although they didn't mention his role.

Pearl and I settled down a short distance away from the counter so that the two women didn't even notice us—the conversation took up all their concentration.

Tracy complained that Alessio wasn't giving her the attention she desired, and perhaps didn't really reciprocate her deep and sincere feelings for him.

"What do I have to do, Sissi?" she asked the older woman. "I'm prepared to do whatever it takes. How can I make Alessio fall in love with me like Leonard did with you? I envy you so much...."

Sissi smiled, and a warm glow spread across her cheeks. "I had to grow and develop, Tracy, to become my best and most beautiful self. But it was so worth it. First, you could do some work on your looks."

Tracy's dark eyes widened. "What's wrong with me? Am I not pretty enough? Is that why he doesn't want me?"

"That's not what I said, sweetie," Sissi replied quickly. "But there's always room for improvement, don't you think? Until you're so beautiful that the man of your dreams just can't resist you, you know what I mean? Of course, it won't happen overnight, but no effort is too great for the right guy, you know?"

Tracy looked like she was about to cry into one of the many glasses behind the bar, but instead she nodded vigorously. "I want to do everything. Alessio simply is my Mr. Right."

Sissi smiled again. "Life is perfect when you've conquered the man of your dreams, I can tell you that much. It's how I feel about Leonard—every morning when I wake up next to him, I have to pinch myself to see if I'm not just dreaming."

"You lucky girl," Tracy said longingly. Her gaze flitted over the guests sitting at the tables in the bar, but apparently no one had a wish that she needed to attend to.

She leaned forward a little. "What should I do to improve my appearance?" she asked, clearly highly motivated.

"Whatever it takes," was Sissi's answer. "Find out what Alessio likes, what attracts him—does he like very slim women or does he fancy fuller figures? What hair color does he prefer? Short or long hair? A bigger bust perhaps? And you can become a master of the art of make-up; I've taken countless courses."

"Oh, okay." Tracy suddenly looked startled.

But Sissi wasn't finished yet. "And you should use the hotel gym regularly—tone and shape your body. And then maybe a small cosmetic procedure or two. A more pointed nose? Whiter teeth. And last but not least, go shopping. I'd be happy to advise you on which clothes would best accentuate your assets."

Tracy held on to the counter. She seemed to have lost her balance, even though she wasn't wearing shoes as high as Sissi's.

"Thank you for your advice," she said in a raspy voice. "It seems I still have a long way to go."

"Don't give up, sweetie," said Sissi. "You can do it."

The barmaid nodded, but looked anything but confident.

"Another unhappy love affair," I said to Pearl.

"Hmm?" She didn't seem to have heard me properly. She was staring out into the darkness of the forest again.

"Have you forgotten?" I said. "We've just had our first experience as love detectives in Vienna, haven't we? But this Alessio—is he really as much of a dreamboat as Tracy thinks he is? I mean, he should make a little effort for her too, shouldn't he? Not just her for him."

"Love is incredibly complicated," Pearl murmured, her tail twitching a little, still not looking at me. I felt as if only her outer shell were sitting next to me.

"Are you all right, Tiny?" I asked worriedly.

9

Before Pearl could give me an answer, a man came striding purposefully towards the bar. He looked first at Sissi, then at Tracy, and finally ordered a small beer from the barmaid.

Sissi said goodbye to her friend. "We'll talk again tomorrow if you'd like, yes? I think Leonard is expecting me." She placed her hand briefly on Tracy's, then stalked out of the bar like a beautiful stork wrapped in green silk.

The man sat down on one of the bar stools and didn't take his eyes off Tracy, who was tapping his beer.

He was perhaps in his mid-thirties, wearing jeans and a black wool sweater, as well as one of those tousled beards that human men like to grow—perhaps to compensate for their otherwise modest body hair.

He had angular features and broad shoulders, and from the way he looked around the bar, he must not have been in here often. A hotel guest who had just arrived, I assumed.

He introduced himself to the barmaid as Richard, complimented her on her traditional dress, which came across as a little awkward, and attempted a winning smile when she placed the beer in front of him.

Maybe he was lonely, I thought to myself, but he was clearly trying very hard to engage Tracy in conversation. First he spoke about the hotel, then Tyrol in general, but he seemed too friendly to me. Tracy chatted to him politely, though as a barmaid she was probably obliged to do so, and she didn't seem to have any real interest in the conversation.

Suddenly Richard lowered his voice, sounding very much like a conspirator, and asked, "Isn't it terrible for you to work here in this hotel, where these two young women have been kidnapped? Or maybe even murdered?"

Tracy had no real answer to that. She just let out a noncommittal sigh.

But Richard continued to probe: "What do you think happened to those women?"

"Are you a true crime fanatic too?" the barmaid blurted out. "Or why would you be interested in it?"

He hesitated briefly. "Yes I am, in a way," he said.

Tracy tried to turn away, even though none of the other bar patrons needed her attention. It seemed she didn't feel like talking about murder or kidnapping.

But Richard wasn't giving up yet. "I've heard that women have disappeared here in the forest before, quite often in fact. And wasn't the last one—before these two sisters—a colleague of yours? A barmaid here at the hotel?"

"How do you know that?" Tracy's dark eyes narrowed suspiciously.

The man merely shrugged his shoulders. "It was in the newspapers."

"But only here in Tyrol, as far as I know," replied Tracy. "And you're German, aren't you? Judging by your accent, anyway."

Richard gave a smile, albeit a little forced. "Seems to me you're a good observer, Tracy. I'm sure you'd be quite talented as an amateur sleuth."

"But I'm not interested in that sort of thing. I don't even watch TV crime dramas—I can't sleep afterwards."

"Understandable," said Richard. "I'm not interested in these murders just for the thrill of it, either. I feel terrible for these poor women who have just dropped off the face of the earth and nobody seems to want to look for them. At least not the police."

"Where there are no bodies, there's not much they can do—at least that's what they're saying. But how did you really find out about my missing colleague?" Tracy could be quite persistent, I realized. Apparently, this Richard had aroused her suspicion, and mine too, by the way. He was somehow ... strange. So tense, as if he had something to hide. I couldn't describe it any better than that.

"I was on vacation here in Tyrol back when your colleague disappeared," the man explained. "About six months ago, that's when it was, wasn't it? I read about it in the local newspaper. And people were talking about it in my hotel, too."

"Mm-hmm," said Tracy. By now she was looking pretty miserable, but didn't seem to have any idea how to end the conversation.

I got to my feet and walked a little closer to the counter. Should I come to the poor woman's aid?

But Richard was already talking again: "That barmaid—her name was Beate, wasn't it?—was having an affair with the hotel manager, if I remember correctly? Leonard Zauner."

"What makes you think that?" Tracy frowned.

"I read it in the newspaper."

"I'm sure it wasn't in the papers," Tracy countered brusquely. Her polite façade was gone by now. She seemed downright repulsed by the man and his curiosity.

But he just shrugged his shoulders again nonchalantly. "Then maybe someone mentioned it in my hotel—I don't remember. But it's true, isn't it?"

Tracy didn't have an answer for him.

"Which hotel did you stay in?" she asked instead.

He shrugged again dismissively. I trotted a little closer so that I could sniff him inconspicuously.

Hmm, he actually did smell very tense. Quite stressed, to be precise.

"You'll have to excuse me, now," said Tracy. "The other guests...." She pointed in the direction of the tables, although no one there had given any sign that they wanted to order anything or pay the bill.

Richard looked demonstratively at his wristwatch. "I'm going to get some sleep," he mumbled. "Nice chatting with you."

She nodded to him. "Please sign your bill for me.

Room number?"

"Twenty-two," he said.

"Thank you."

Tracy printed out the bill, he signed it, and as grumpy as her "thank you" sounded, he probably hadn't given her a tip. Or not enough of one.

That was another thing I didn't really understand yet. Sometimes the two-leggeds paid exactly what was asked of them without saying a word, whereas on other occasions, they haggled as if it were a sport in which they were trying to win a medal. And sometimes, such as when they were eating or drinking, they voluntarily paid more, which they then called a tip. Their physical well-being was clearly particularly important to them—just like it was with Pearl, my little glutton. Except, of course, she never tipped. Yes, we pets were almost always fed for free, even by strangers and in restaurants. Which once again showed just how important we were to the two-leggeds.

"Quite a lot of true crime fans here in the hotel," I said to Pearl.

"Mm-hmm. A place like this Killer's Wood with all the missing women must have a magical attraction for them. Good that we're here too—we're urgently needed, it seems to me."

I panted in agreement. At least Pearl seemed to be interested in the case again now, and had returned to her favorite role as a velvet-pawed detective instead of staring holes into the night. That reassured me a little.

10

The next morning, I was awoken by Tim. To be precise, I was already in the twilight state between sleeping and waking, otherwise I might not have noticed those words of his that heralded the end of our peaceful vacation.

I was lying on the rug, feeling Pearl's barely perceptible weight on my front paw, which she had once again turned into a pillow, and enjoying the morning silence. Until Tim turned around up on the bed and addressed Victoria: "Are you awake, my darling?"

"Mm-hmm," was the answer. "What time is it? Is it breakfast time already?"

"Yes. But listen, sweetie, I've been thinking—"

When a human uttered these words, it often meant nothing good. I had already learned that much in my dealings with the two-leggeds.

Perhaps Victoria had had similar experiences. In any case, she sat up, leaned herself against the head of the bed and stared at Tim, a little startled.

He smiled, but looked quite nervous. "I ... well, I can't get this Henrik Engel out of my head. How desperately he's looking for his wife."

"For her sister rather," commented Pearl, who had now lifted her head from my paw and seemed to be awake. I assumed it was the word *breakfast* that had brought her out of her sleep.

"Yes, the poor man," Victoria said to Tim. "Hopefully everything will turn out okay and the two women will reappear unharmed."

Tim took her hand and squeezed it gently. "I've been up half the night thinking about him—and the missing women, of course. Maybe they haven't just gone into hiding after all, but are in serious danger."

"Or already dead," muttered Victoria. "Horrible idea, but I'm afraid it might be true."

I knew that Victoria had also been up half the night. I had awoken a few times because she was tossing and turning in bed, until I finally gave her a few wet ear kisses to calm her down.

This earned me the usual "Ugh, Athos, stop that!"—but Victoria had fallen asleep after that. My ear kisses *worked*, even if they weren't properly appreciated.

"What if Fabienne and Natalia aren't dead yet, but their lives are hanging by a thread?" Tim continued. "If they're being held captive somewhere by a psychopathic serial killer who wants them—"

"Don't, Tim!" Victoria interrupted him. "I don't even want to imagine that."

"But don't you understand, darling? We mustn't abandon them. We might be able to help Henrik find them alive, after all. He may be a die-hard true crime fan, but we're much more experienced than he is even so. And we have Athos and Pearl. These two have proven so many times that they're ... oh, I don't know. That they're excellent detectives, as crazy as that sounds."

"And what does that mean for us now?" asked Victoria. "That we should forget about our vacation and throw ourselves into this case?"

Tim's lips quirked at the corners. "I ... well, as long as you don't mind. I'm just imagining how I would feel in the situation Henrik is currently in. If *you* were missing, I would do everything I could to find you again, and would certainly appreciate any help I could get!"

Victoria nodded slowly. "I'd feel the same way," she said.

"Then it's okay by you if we offer Henrik our help?"

"I guess we'll have to. We'll just ... postpone our vacation, okay? I mean, you still have to keep studying for your exam, I suppose? Right?"

"Yes, of course. I'm certainly not going to throw my studies away. And you should definitely carry on with your cross-country skiing lessons. You enjoy them, don't you?"

"They're great fun, actually. Just like sledging with Athos."

"That's good. Just because we're helping Henrik with his investigation, doesn't mean we can't still have a bit of fun. By all means! And not just out in the forest." He winked seductively at Victoria.

She laughed, leaned forward and gave him a big kiss.

My two-leggeds had the opportunity to put their new plan into action at breakfast. They didn't even have to actively and explicitly offer Henrik their help, because we had barely settled down at one of the rustic wooden tables in the hotel restaurant when the man was already standing there in front of us. He had several folders and a large, tattered notebook tucked under his arm, held a cup of coffee in his other hand and asked in a pleading voice if he could show Victoria and Tim something for a moment.

They offered him a seat at the table, and Tim tried to explain that he and Victoria had reconsidered, and changed their minds about working on the case.

But he didn't much of a chance, because Henrik immediately let out a passionate "Thank you!" and then started talking like a waterfall again, just as he had done the day before.

He sat down on the vacant chair at the table and placed the tattered notebook in front of him as if it were his greatest treasure. He stroked the cover, which was a dark blue and decorated with leafy tendrils, as if he were caressing the fur of his favorite pet. Or perhaps I should say, the skin of his favorite human. Natalia's skin, who—as we were about to find out—was the owner of this notebook.

"*Natalia's Casebook*. That's what she called it, you know," he explained to Tim and Victoria. "She loved to give things pretty names."

He sighed. "She was, no, she *is* ... because she simply has to be alive! She is such an imaginative woman, bubbling over with vitality and joie de vivre, you know?"

"Yes," said Tim, "but you wanted to tell us about an important discovery, didn't you?"

"What? Oh, yes, of course." Henrik blinked, as if he needed to push aside the glorified image of his sister-in-law that had probably just appeared before his eyes.

"I went through all our case files and notes here on the Killer's Wood again tonight. I just couldn't sleep, you know."

You could see from his face that he was telling the truth: his eyes were red, surrounded by deep dark circles, and his skin looked sallow and flabby.

But he was also a fighter. He wouldn't give up, I told myself, not until he knew for sure what had happened to Natalia. As for Fabienne, his wife—well, I wouldn't have placed any bets that he would take similarly desperate measures for her.

I didn't know the woman, but I felt sorry for her. Being married to a man who loved and desired her sister more than her must have felt terrible. Once again—as happened so often—I was glad to be a dog and not a human.

Henrik carefully opened Natalia's casebook and turned to the last few pages. "Natalia had made a discovery that I didn't know about until now. Normally, all three of us always shared our findings with each other as quickly as we could, so I assume that Natalia must have made these notes shortly before she disappeared. She didn't date her entries consistently, you know."

"And what did she find out?" asked Victoria, who was probably just as curious as I was.

A triumphant smile flitted across Henrik's tired features. "I've already told you that all the women who have disappeared here over the years—seven in total that we know of—had a connection to this hotel. They were either guests at the Alpenrose or worked here. The very first to lose her life in the forest was the wife of the owner—Leonard Zauner. You've already met him, I presume? Eight years ago, Lucy Zauner set off on a hike and fell into a ravine. But she was apparently quite experienced in the local terrain. There was neither a storm nor was she caught in the dark, or anything of the kind, that might have explained her death."

"The police assumed it was an accident?" asked Tim.

Henrik nodded. "Officially, anyway. Allegedly, suicide was also considered, as far as we've been able to reconstruct after so many years. But Leonard Zauner is convinced that it was an accident—if he talks about it at all."

"Poor man," Victoria said. "How could he stay here and continue to run this hotel when he lost his wife in such a terrible way?"

"Everything here must remind him of her," Henrik agreed. "They ran the hotel together for such a long time."

He groaned softly, but then the hint of a smile stole

across his face. "It's so good to be able to talk to you about this case. Can we be on a first-name basis? Among true crime colleagues, as it were?"

Victoria nodded, then Tim did too.

Henrik continued without taking a breath: "I haven't known you for very long, but you seem so trustworthy. I would really give anything for you to help me find Natalia and Fabienne. If it's a fee you want, I'm sure I can raise a handsome sum—"

Victoria raised her hands defensively. "That's really not necessary."

She glanced at Tim, then she added: "My boyfriend and I have decided that we want to help you as much as we can. We ourselves would be grateful for any help if we were in a similar situation."

"Oh, thank God! You don't know what this means to me!" Henrik's voice sounded rough.

He cleared his throat, then continued: "But now I have to get to the point. So then, Natalia's discovery was this: All the women who allegedly had accidents in the forest, who supposedly committed suicide or simply disappeared ... Natalia found out that they all—without exception, you understand?—had a connection to Leonard Zauner! So perhaps you're wrong to feel sorry for the man, Victoria."

11

"A connection?" Victoria repeated blankly. "What exactly do you mean? That all these women knew Leonard Zauner, or worked for him?"

"It's more than that," exclaimed Henrik. The next moment he was putting his index finger to his lips and looking furtively around the dining room. "We have to be careful. He mustn't know that we know—otherwise we'll put ourselves in danger too."

"I'm afraid you've lost me," said Tim, a little confused.

"Leonard Zauner was romantically involved with all of these women," Henrik whispered. "He was married to the first one, and if what Natalia wrote in her notebook is true, he was either officially involved or having an affair with all of the other six victims. That really can't be a coincidence, I would think."

Both Tim and Victoria looked impressed. Tim even clicked his tongue. And the tiny one sitting next to me commented, "Wow, if that's not a hot lead!"

Victoria finally asked: "How did Natalia get this information? Did she write anything about it in her notebook?"

"Unfortunately she didn't," said Henrik, "but she was so very intuitive, you know? Fabienne always proceeded in a logical and structured way, collected facts, evaluated them like a mathematician; and that wasn't a bad method—I really don't want to say that. My head works in a very similar way. But Natalia—"

A dreamy expression came into his eyes. "She was an intuitive genius. She perceived things that other people overlooked. Sometimes you even got the impression that she was somehow clairvoyant. Although I don't believe in that, of course," he added quickly.

"And was she often right with her ... intuition, with her hunches?" asked Victoria.

"Right on the money."

Henrik's eyes began to light up. "She was ... she *is* unique. Clever, most amazingly wise, I would say. And beautiful. Everyone loves her."

I couldn't help noticing that Victoria found this comment just as strange as I did. Didn't Henrik realize how inappropriate it was for him to rave about his sister-in-law like this?

"Is Natalia married too?" Victoria asked him. "Or does she have a boyfriend?"

A few seconds passed before Henrik could answer. "No, she's—I don't think she wanted to commit. She got married young, but that was before I met her. Her husband disappeared one day and was never seen again. And since then, as far as I know, she's remained single."

Both Tim and Victoria raised their eyebrows at this statement.

"That's ... interesting," Pearl commented. "The husband also disappeared?"

Henrik continued: "That's how the Crime Sisters were

born, you know, why the two sisters became amateur detectives in the first place. The first case they investigated was the disappearance of Natalia's husband. Unfortunately, they have still not been able to solve it. Their failure gnawed at Natalia, I think, even though she hardly ever talked about it."

"So we have a man who vanished into thin air many years ago," Pearl observed, "and now seven missing women here in the forest. Plus the two Crime Sisters."

"Well, I can't imagine there's a connection," I said. "Natalia's husband disappearing just explains why she became a snoop. That's all, I think."

"Yes, possibly." Pearl began to groom herself. She wet one of her paws with the tip of her tiny pink tongue and ran it carefully over her ears—a sight that would have melted even the hardest of hearts. It was easy to forget what a bloodthirsty little monster Tiny was.

"A challenging case, then," she continued with immense satisfaction. "We probably won't be bored with this investigation."

"Bored? That's your biggest worry?" I asked incredulously.

She looked at me impassively. "We don't want to end up like the humans, do we? Well, most of them anyway. The same routine day in, day out, and then some of them return to a home in the evening where not even a cat lives with them."

"Really pitiful," I muttered. "But to come back to the case: A few of the missing women really could have died of natural causes, in an accident here in the mountains. Or perhaps they actually took their own lives because, um ... they didn't have a cat to serve?"

I don't know why I said that—Pearl sometimes brought out a crazy streak in me.

"Now you're just exaggerating," she said. "People don't love us that much. Well, exceptions prove the rule, of course, but...."

"Yes, yes, okay," I interrupted her.

Victoria did me the favor of distracting us by addressing Henrik again. She asked him for details about the alleged murder victims that he, his wife and his sister-in-law had turned up in their investigation.

Henrik was able to give her the information without having to consult his files. He had apparently really familiarized himself with the cases.

"Lucy Zauner, the hotelier's wife, was the first to die in strange circumstances," he began. "I've already told you all about that. Almost two years later, a cook who had only been working here at the Alpenrose for a few months simply disappeared. According to Natalia's notes, she was carrying on a secret affair with Leonard Zauner."

"This relationship can't have been all that secret," said Tim, "if your sister-in-law was able to find out about it years later."

Henrik shrugged his shoulders. "I'm just giving you what Natalia wrote down. I'm not saying she was infallible—"

He broke off. I was sitting very close to him so as not to miss a single detail of what he was saying, and he suddenly reached out his hand and started stroking my head. It came as a surprise, but still I enjoyed it. He knew how to caress me—not too gently, not too firmly, and without pulling my hair out. That was by no means par for the course with humans.

He mentioned the name of the missing cook, but I immediately forgot it because I was so distracted by the pleasant massage. *Shame on me.* Something like that shouldn't happen to a proper detective!

After this woman, more two-leggeds had gone missing from the hotel at short intervals.

Tim wrote down what Henrik had to say, but I had to rely on my memory to store the information—not that these details mattered much at this stage of the investigation. So far, they were just names for which I had neither a face nor a smell. Still, I was tormented by the idea that all these humans had perhaps been murdered in a horrible way.

"We need to concentrate on Fabienne and Natalia first," said Pearl. "And maybe the woman before that. With the older cases, it will be virtually impossible to find any evidence now."

Her eyes suddenly brightened. "Unless Moonshadow can track down their corpses in the forest."

"We shouldn't get our hopes up," I said. "If these women really are dead, but they haven't been found in all these years, then the murderer may have buried their bodies deep or thrown them somewhere in a ravine where not even a lynx can get to them."

"Moonshadow is certainly very good off-road," said Pearl. "And he can question the trees. We really must visit him again soon."

Her voice sounded like she was once again preaching to me about her beloved cat goddess, or how humans were obsessed with cats as superior beings. Not exactly the kind of topics that made my heart beat faster. And as for how she was obsessed with Moonshadow ... I didn't much like that either.

Because of our brief conversation, Pearl and I missed out on more details about the missing women, so I can only tell you about the last two victims.

Around six months ago, Beate Krüger, a barmaid at the hotel, had disappeared without a trace, and around four months before that, a female hotel guest named Sarah Schneider had either left without paying her bill—and never arrived back at her home town in Germany—or she had also been kidnapped or murdered.

Henrik explained to Tim and Victoria that Leonard Zauner had had a love affair with both of these women. However, Beate, the barmaid, had been single and at least her work colleagues knew about the affair, while Sarah Schneider had been a married woman and Leonard had never officially admitted that anything had happened between them.

"He is quite the ladies' man," Henrik concluded, "even though he looks rather staid. Do you think, Victoria—

as a psychologist—that he is somehow disturbed? Could he have psychopathic traits?"

"I've only exchanged a few words with the man so far," Victoria replied, "and unfortunately you can't tell whether someone is a psychopath or not from a bit of small talk."

"Yes, well, I realize that," said Henrik. He raised his eyebrows sheepishly.

"And not every psychopath is violent, let alone ends up becoming a serial killer," added Victoria.

Henrik nodded. Apparently he'd heard about that too.

12

Henrik got up, went over to the breakfast buffet and came back with a steaming cup of coffee.

"What do we do now? How can we convict Zauner, collect evidence against him—"

"Not so fast," said Tim. "It's far too early to commit to any one suspect."

Henrik looked astonished. "But you agree with me that it can't possibly be a coincidence? I mean that all the women who have disappeared were involved with this man."

"We can't say whether these seven women you've just told us about were really the only ones who have disappeared in the forest over the last few years, can we?" Victoria objected. "You and your partners may only have been able to identify those who were in contact with this hotel and its owner. That could be because this is where you focused your investigation. Perhaps the list of possible victims is much longer, and not limited to guests or employees of the Alpenrose. I really hope that more women aren't affected, but it's possible."

Henrik didn't say anything in reply. He took a sip of coffee, but it burned his tongue. "Ouch, that's hot!" he gasped.

Victoria asked him: "Did you also interrogate people

outside the hotel? In other accommodation nearby? Or in the villages, at the lift stations...?"

"No, we'd only just started." Henrik sounded a little defiant.

"I'm really not trying to criticize you," Victoria reassured him. "I'm just saying that we shouldn't ignore other possibilities."

"Yeah, okay...."

"I'd like to recap exactly what happened on the day Fabienne and Natalia disappeared," Tim interposed.

Pearl jumped onto his lap. "I'd like to know that too." Her whiskers twitched, and she now looked extremely focused—as she had in the past when she had taken on the role of master detective. The case had apparently captured her now, which was preferable to her sitting absently staring out of the window.

"Natalia was the first to leave," said Henrik. "The three of us had, um, been talking—until she suddenly left the room, announcing that she wanted to stretch her legs a bit. When she didn't return, I think Fabienne went to look for her."

"You think?" asked Victoria.

Henrik pressed his hands against his temples and looked very unhappy. "I did mention that we had an argument. Fabienne left the room shortly after Natalia did—she went into the small closet in our suite, which we had turned into the operations center. I left her alone ... but later, when I went to check on her, she was gone. And her winter boots and jacket were missing, so

I assumed she'd gone outside."

"And neither of them ever returned." That came from Tim. It was more of a statement than a question.

Henrik nodded. "I went to dinner then. Alone. And afterwards I went to the bar, and when I finally returned to our suite, Fabienne's luggage was gone. I ran straight to Natalia's room, of course, because I thought my wife might have moved in with her, but she wasn't there. And Natalia's luggage was gone as well."

"You had a key to your sister-in-law's room?"

"No—I asked a chambermaid who was doing the evening room service on our floor to unlock the door for me. I explained to her that I was looking for Natalia, and for my wife, who had both just disappeared. She was super correct, called her boss first, but she probably gave the green light, so the maid finally unlocked the door for me. And as I said, Natalia's luggage was gone too."

"And so you assumed they had both gone back home?" That came from Tim.

Henrik nodded with a frustrated expression.

"What was your argument about?" asked Victoria.

"What does it matter?" Henrik suddenly looked angry.

Victoria didn't really have an answer to that, but I got the impression that she wasn't ruling out Henrik himself as a possible suspect. This was good detective work, as we had learned from our friend Chief Inspector Oskar Nüring—but I really couldn't imagine that Henrik, this unfortunate man who had asked us so desperately for help, would have done anything to his wife.

"He probably wouldn't have done anything to his sister-in-law," Pearl commented. "More likely to his wife."

Apparently I had spoken my thoughts for her to hear.

"What do you mean?" I asked.

"Isn't that obvious? I think he loved Natalia more than his own wife. He's always talking about how wonderful and brilliant she is, staring at her photos and so on. Maybe he even had an affair with her?"

"Do you really think she would have done that to her sister?"

"No idea. As we know, the humans are capable of anything, aren't they?"

I couldn't disagree with that.

Tim came to Victoria's aid: "Listen Henrik, no offense, but if we're going to work together, we can't keep secrets from each other. And after all, your argument was apparently so heated that you thought the two sisters might have left because of it, so it must have been more than just a minor disagreement. That much is obvious."

Henrik groaned. "It really wasn't worth mentioning. No big deal at all. Fabienne can just be very temperamental, and...." He jutted out his chin rather pugnaciously. "I really don't want to discuss my marriage with you! *I* haven't done anything to Natalia or Fabienne, and if you're seriously considering it, then you're just wasting valuable time! Don't you two ever argue?"

Rarely, I could have told him. My two-leggeds were

both level-headed people. They often enjoyed a good argument with each other, but they never got really loud or so hurtful that one of them felt compelled to simply run away—as Fabienne had obviously done. And her sister as well, whether she was Henrik's secret lover or not.

13

When breakfast at last was finished, Victoria suggested that we first interview some of the hotel staff.

Henrik was immediately on fire with the idea. "Which room could we use as an interrogation room? The library, perhaps? There's hardly ever anything going on there, or so it seems to me. And how do we want to go about it? According to the good cop, bad cop strategy? And the third of us would then be...?"

"I don't think we should have the three of us talking," Victoria interrupted him. "And I wouldn't carry out interrogations either—otherwise people will immediately go on the defensive and we won't find out anything."

"Well, me and the girls, we have always interviewed people together," Henrik replied. "If you come out as a true crime fan, you mostly get an understanding for your curiosity. So many people love crime novels, murder mysteries and investigations."

"Okay, it shouldn't turn into an interrogation though," said Tim, "but remain on an informal basis."

Henrik nodded and shrugged his shoulders sheepishly. "Admittedly, it was usually Natalia or Fabienne who did the talking during our, er, interviews. I always tended to stay in the background. People are more likely to open up to a woman, I think."

Tim looked at Victoria. "Shall we try it with the three of us? I think we'll be accepted more easily if Henrik asks the questions. After all, his wife and sister-in-law are affected."

Before Victoria could reply, Henrik nodded again, this time more eagerly. "I'll just introduce you two as fellow fans of True Crime. How about that? It's not far from the truth."

Pearl liked the term *true crime*. "You and I, Athos, are of course also true crime experts, not only top detectives," she explained. "Why did we miss out on that until now?"

"Does it matter what we call ourselves? Do you want to have business cards printed?" I joked. "To impress your new boyfriend?"

"My new boyfriend?"

"Moonshadow. You've been very unfocused since you met him."

"Not true at all," protested Pearl.

Oh my goodness, had I really just said that? What was I doing? I was behaving just like the two-leggeds when they were jealous! What was wrong with me?

"It's important what we call ourselves," Pearl explained to me. "It's about having the right self-image. That's vital if you want to achieve anything in life."

Where had she picked that up from? It sounded like one of those self-help gurus we occasionally saw on TV. Not too often, because the focus of our viewing program was still on murder and everything that went with it.

"And what do you want to achieve?" I asked.

I should have kept my snout shut.

"I want to be the best, that's for sure."

"The best what?"

"Cat detective." She tilted her head. "Although, come to think of it, we can easily compete with the humans too."

"So the best detective—in the whole universe?" I suggested.

As is so often the case, my sarcasm was completely lost on Pearl.

"Yes. Why not?" she said.

She jumped off Tim's lap and meowed loudly. "Let's get going!" she said, and then: "Who are we going to question first?"

Our two-leggeds decided to start with Tracy—simply because she was the first member of staff we came across when we left the restaurant.

She wasn't on duty, because the bar was closed in the morning, and she let herself be persuaded to have a chat in the library without much resistance.

Henrik explained that he wanted to take the search for Natalia and Fabienne into his own hands now that the police had given up, and Tracy understood, just as Tim had suspected.

The young barmaid even seemed to be enjoying the

attention she was receiving. She told us everything she had heard about Natalia and Fabienne's stay at the hotel, but unfortunately she couldn't provide any information that we didn't already know.

However, the picture she drew of the two women did not match the one we had gained from Henrik. In Tracy's eyes, Fabienne had undoubtedly been the more interesting and friendly woman, while she seemed to have perceived Natalia as rather arrogant, even if she didn't say so directly.

Finally, she seemed to have an idea, because she suddenly slapped her forehead with her hand. "Maybe you should talk to that Richard Schöndorf from Room 22—he's a true crime fan too, I think—although kind of weird. Not as nice as you." She smiled. "He tried to pump me for information last night."

Victoria scribbled something in the little notebook she had placed in front of her. I assumed it was the name and room number of the man Pearl and I had seen in the bar last night.

Tracy fell silent for a moment and her brow furrowed. "He knew things that weren't made public, about a colleague of mine who disappeared in the woods a few months ago. You questioned me about her too, Mr. Engel," she said, turning to Henrik. "That is—no. It was your wife who did, I think."

"Which colleague are you talking about? Beate Krüger?" asked Tim.

"Yes, exactly."

"She disappeared from the hotel," said Henrik. "Just like Natalia and Fabienne did. So we have to assume the same perpetrator."

Tracy blinked away a tear. "She was such a nice girl, Beate. But before her, many others have vanished in our forest, or had accidents. They were always women, but I didn't know them because I wasn't working here at the time."

Her eyes wandered from Henrik to Tim, then to Victoria. "I'm afraid I can't help you any further, can I? I'm sure you already know everything I've told you. You'd better talk to my Alessio, our night porter here at the hotel. He's a very clever man and he's been working here for a long time. He doesn't miss anything that happens in the hotel, especially at night and in secret."

"Alessio is your boyfriend?" Victoria asked warmly.

Whereupon Tracy's cheeks suddenly darkened. "Yeah, well ... I don't really know."

She hung her head and suddenly smelled very sad. "He's a very special man, really very intelligent and attractive. And I'm just—oh, I don't know. A silly little goose. Even if I do want to work on myself, yes, I certainly will! Sissi, our head housekeeper, is giving me tips on how I can improve. I would do anything for Alessio. But will I ever be good enough for him?"

She swallowed and averted her eyes. "Besides, he needs his freedom," she whispered. "He's said that more than once."

Victoria opened her mouth, but then closed it again

without saying anything. I got the impression that she took an immediate dislike to this Alessio just like I had done before.

The question I had to ask myself was whether this guy had anything like a heart. Tracy might not have been an intellectual, but she certainly wasn't stupid, and her heart was in the right place, you could tell that right away. She was friendly and helpful, but as far as her self-confidence was concerned, she could have done with a little coaching from Pearl.

Victoria carefully took the young woman's hand. "Please don't let anyone tell you that you're not good enough, Tracy. Okay?"

"Do you really think so?" whispered the barmaid.

"Absolutely! And thank you very much for your help with our case. We'll talk to this Richard Schöndorf from Room 22 whom you mentioned. And with Alessio too," she added in a much cooler tone.

14

The next hotel employee Henrik and my two-leggeds interviewed was Sissi Fassbender, the head of housekeeping and the current girlfriend of the hotelier.

Henrik made the same brief statement with which he had opened the previous conversation—namely that he wanted to take the search for Natalia and Fabienne into his own hands now that the police, in his opinion, had given up and would probably do nothing more to rescue the two women.

"Do you think they're still alive?" Sissi asked quite bluntly.

"I hope so. I won't allow myself to think otherwise!" exclaimed Henrik. "Or else I would ... oh no, I don't even want to imagine that. I'd be lost without her."

He didn't say who exactly he meant by *her*. Natalia? Fabienne? Both of them?

Victoria asked the housekeeper the following question: "Did you perhaps observe anything a week ago—here in the hotel or in the surrounding area—that seemed strange to you? Or even suspicious? Anything that could be connected to the disappearance of the two women? After all, they're not the first two to go missing. I'm sure you know that."

Sissi nodded slowly. "Leonard is terribly worried about it. Every time I go jogging in the woods or even just leave the hotel on my own, he reproaches me. He means well, of course, I do know that, and it's a terrible burden on him..."

"In what way?" Tim asked. "Was he personally acquainted with Natalia or Fabienne?"

We all knew by now that he had been in some sort of relationship with the women who had disappeared in the past, but that was probably not the case with the two most recent missing women. Or was it? Had the hotel owner perhaps also started a relationship with Natalia, who was single? Even if it was just a fleeting affair, as she had only been at the hotel for a few days?

"Or with Fabienne?" said Pearl. "Which would have been far worse."

Apparently I had been thinking out loud again. Or did Pearl know me so well by now that she could read my thoughts from my expression?

Sissi directed her answer to Henrik, even though Tim had asked the question. "Leonard has barely exchanged a word with your wife or sister-in-law. He greeted all three of you personally on arrival, I assume, as he does with all the hotel guests, but beyond that—" She shook her head. "I don't think he had any other contact with them. But it's clear that their disappearance still weighs on him, isn't it? Leonard is a wonderful man. This terrible thing affects him as it does all of us. The poor women, you can't even imagine what they might be going through.... But of course Leonard also has the reputation of his hotel and our entire region at stake. Who wants to spend their vacation in a *Killer's Wood*?"

"Lots of two-leggeds," Pearl interjected. "It's bound to attract more curious onlookers and true crime fans than scare off vacationers."

I agreed with her, and the hotel was indeed well frequented. There certainly weren't many empty rooms.

Henrik blurted out the next question: "The first woman to disappear here in the forest was Leonard Zauner's wife, wasn't she?"

Sissi nodded with a sorrowful expression. "She didn't disappear, she had an accident while hiking. But yes, that was a heavy blow for Leonard. My poor darling."

"Was it a happy marriage?" Henrik continued, unabashedly.

"What are you trying to say?" This time Sissi looked a little irritated. "He did everything for her, while she—no, I'm not going to talk ill of a dead woman! And none of us are perfect, are we? Lucy was a little overwhelmed with Maxim, their only child, and the boy took years afterwards to get over his mother's death. He was in therapy for a long time, even suicidal. I was just an employee here at the hotel at the time, but I felt terribly sorry for him, and I've tried to be a kind of surrogate mother to him ever since."

Her gaze wandered around the room, a little dreamily, until she realized that she was lost in her memories. She cleared her throat and looked at Victoria, who seemed to be her favorite person to talk to. Perhaps she assumed that a woman was most likely to understand her.

"Maxim has grown into a fine young man," she said, "although still very shy, you know. He hasn't had a relationship of his own yet, even though he's now twenty years old. But I don't think he's missing out on anything."

"And Leonard hasn't remarried?" Victoria asked. She probably wanted to know how he had got over his wife's death over the years.

"Oh, I don't believe he has been living like a monk," Sissi admitted with a smile. "I'm not fooling myself about that. But I don't think he'd found the right one yet."

She suddenly beamed. "Lucky for me, isn't it? Now a happy ending awaits us both."

"Then you're engaged?" Victoria replied.

Sissi's smile faded. "Not yet. Our relationship is ... still quite young. But I think he'll ask me to marry him soon. As a woman, you can just sense it."

"Then I wish you both all the best for the future," said Victoria kindly.

"Thank you!" Her beaming smile returned.

As with Tracy before her, Tim and Victoria didn't say a word to Sissi about the discovery that Natalia had recorded in her casebook shortly before her disappearance—namely that all the women who had gone missing or suffered accidents in the Killer's Wood had been in a close relationship with Leonard Zauner.

Henrik, however, was not so subtle. "Mr. Zauner didn't just lose his wife, he was also close to the other women who disappeared here over the years," he said to Sissi.

"What makes you think that?" she asked. One of her eyebrows moved towards her hairline.

"Isn't it true?"

Sissi stared at the man. "I have no idea. I didn't snoop into Leonard's business—but apparently you did."

"Yes, we are quite thorough in our investigations," Henrik countered.

The relaxed atmosphere in the room was suddenly gone. Sissi felt visibly attacked and Henrik smelled quite belligerent.

"And in these so-called investigations, you focused on Leonard of all people?" asked Sissi. "Or did you scrutinize everyone here in the hotel in the same way?"

She gave herself the answer straight away, now in a decidedly cool tone of voice. "The three of you certainly couldn't have done that in such a short time."

"It's true, even if you don't like it," said Henrik. "Your Leonard is a womanizer ... if not worse."

Sissi didn't say another word. She stood up, turned her back on us and left the library without saying goodbye.

None of our two-leggeds stopped her, but Tim immediately turned to Henrik as soon as she had gone. "Was that really necessary? What do you hope to achieve this way? She'll shut herself off completely and won't speak to us again."

Henrik shrugged his shoulders. "I'm not here to make friends. I want to find out the truth and to do that I just had to lure our witness out of her shell a little. And I hit the bull's eye with my question, don't you realize that? She knows very well that Leonard was involved with these women. Maybe it was news to her that he had a connection with *all of them,* and of course she loves him and wants to protect him. But she was also scared, surely that didn't escape your notice?"

"Well, she didn't seem very scared to me," said Tim.

"Ahh, you have to look more closely. Read between the lines. Hear the unsaid."

"Hear the unsaid?" Tim looked half amused, half irritated.

"I'm not Natalia," Henrik said. "My intuition is nowhere near as good, but I could sense that Sissi was scared. Count on it, man!"

"If you say so," Tim muttered.

Henrik responded: "Don't you realize that she could also be in danger? She's Leonard Zauner's new love. She could be his next victim. It's our duty to not let it come to that!"

"We really shouldn't jump to conclusions so quickly," Victoria intervened in the conversation.

She had a better grip on herself than her boyfriend; she didn't seem angry that Henrik had taken such a heavy-handed approach, although she certainly didn't like it any more than Tim did.

"Jump to conclusions?" Henrik repeated. "Well, I

think Natalia was right with her suspicions. As always! Leonard Zauner is our man, I tell you. And I have experience in these matters."

He seemed to have forgotten that Tim and Victoria had far more experience with murders than he did, but both were polite enough not to rub his nose in it.

But Tim said: "If Leonard Zauner really was our man, wouldn't that also mean, in your opinion, that he had something going on with your wife? Or with your sister-in-law? Or why else would he have done something to them?"

This question caught Henrik off guard. He opened his mouth, croaked something unintelligible, but then slumped down in his chair as if someone had let all the air out of him. Tim was quite capable of being blunt as well when he felt it was necessary.

15

In the afternoon, Victoria had another cross-country skiing lesson with Karl.

The weather was pretty nasty today—from Pearl's perspective at least. An icy wind was blowing and the temperature had dropped significantly compared to the previous day. As a dog, or even as a cat, you don't need complicated technical measuring devices like humans do to be able to tell. You can simply feel it when you put your nose to the wind.

I assumed that Pearl would prefer to stay in the warm suite with Tim in this weather rather than go cross-country skiing, but to my surprise she was the first one in the anteroom when Victoria was making the final preparations for her training session.

"We have to meet Moonshadow again," Tiny explained to me. "I'm sure he's been busy investigating for us, with his tree friends and all that."

"I hope so too," I said, "but I could meet him on my own. I'll find him. Or he'll find me if he wants to."

In fact, I had my doubts as to whether I—or anyone else—could have tracked down the lynx if he didn't want to be found. The answer was probably no.

"I'm coming with you," Pearl decided, and as we trotted alongside Karl and Victoria to the start of the trail, I had the feeling that I had a completely new cat next to me. She strutted along as if this forest were her very own territory and as if neither the brisk wind nor the cold could harm her. Not to mention the mud we had to trudge through in places.

Victoria used her cross-country skiing lesson today primarily to subject Karl to a bit of an interrogation. Of course, she was gentle and friendly, as was her way, so he willingly provided her the information. The two of them almost seemed like old friends to me. Yesterday's training session had probably been very enjoyable and successful, even if Pearl and I had missed most of it.

"You must work for guests at the Alpenrose a lot, don't you, Karl?" Victoria began her line of questioning.

To which he replied in the affirmative. "As the hotel is so ideally located on the cross-country trail, many guests try this kind of skiing as a matter of course," he said. "And most of them start off with an instructor—me." He grinned, exposing his gleaming, white and very straight teeth.

"And in summer, I'm a hiking guide," he went on. "The Alpenrose offers guided tours twice a week, which I lead. But of course I'm also available for guests from other hotels."

"In that case, you certainly know the Alpenrose and the people who work there very well," said Victoria.

"Yes, of course," said Karl. Then he remembered that Victoria had actually come to go cross-country skiing. He climbed into the track next to her and urged her to get going.

She obeyed, of course, and—as far as I could tell as a non-cross-country skier—was already doing quite well on the thin and unwieldy boards.

"Who among the staff has actually been at the hotel long enough?" she asked a few minutes later, when we had already followed the trail a little way into the forest.

"Long enough for...?" asked Karl.

Victoria smiled sheepishly. "Excuse me, please. I can't get the two missing women out of my head. And Henrik Engel, their husband and brother-in-law respectively, has asked me and my friend for help in his search for them."

"Are you police officers, private detectives or something like that?" Karl asked in amazement.

Victoria's smile widened. "Well, not exactly. But we've been involved in a few murder cases in the past, albeit involuntarily. And we were able to help solve them. In other words, Athos and Pearl were actually—"

"Wow," exclaimed Karl, "that sounds incredible."

"I know. Oh!" one of Victoria's skis got stuck and she almost lost her balance.

But Karl grabbed her by the arm in time and caught her.

"Thank you," she gasped, and I wondered again why on earth you would strap such cumbersome things to your paws—er, feet—that you first had to learn to walk with like a newborn puppy.

But Victoria didn't give up on her discreet interrogation because of this mishap.

"To get back to my question," she began as soon as she had covered a few meters without further difficulty.

Pearl and I were able to keep up her pace easily. All in all, she was hardly moving any faster than if she had been walking.

The tiny one was staring holes in the forest and only seemed to be listening with half an ear to what Victoria and Karl were saying. But luckily, I was paying attention.

"Oh right," said Karl, "you wanted to know who's been working at the hotel long enough ... and could possibly have had something to do with the missing women? Is that what you're getting at? You don't seriously believe someone from the Alpenrose could be a murderer, do you?"

"Don't you think that's possible?" she rejoined.

"Well, if you ask me so directly—no! I've known these people forever."

"So that means you've been working for the hotel for a long time?" asked Victoria. She put on a very innocent smile.

Karl stopped abruptly and plunged one of his ski poles into the snow like a lance.

"I've been working here in this region for almost fifteen years," he replied, though I couldn't tell if he was smiling or baring his teeth. It was a mixture of both. His tone, however, remained friendly.

"But I assure you," he added emphatically, "that I do not sneak through the forest and ambush any women.

Or murder them right here on the trail!"

He pulled such a crazy face that Victoria had to laugh.

"No offense," she said, "I'm just gathering facts. I'm not accusing anyone."

"Not yet," said Karl. "Do use your arms! You're not carrying these sticks for fun!"

"Oops, I forgot all about them."

"Because you're not really on the ball."

"That's true ... but there are two lives at stake." She paused. "So apart from you, who else has been working for the Alpenrose for, say, around eight years? Or directly at the hotel?"

Karl eyed her critically. I couldn't tell whether he was bothered by Victoria's questions or just the fact that she wasn't paying enough attention to her cross-country skiing.

He gave her an answer after all: "Well, there's Sissi, the head housekeeper. Alessio, the night porter. Cäcilia, who works in the kitchen. A few of the other employees have also been here for a few years, but I couldn't say exactly how long. And then of course there's the family. So, let's keep moving, shall we? You're certainly not paying me to stand around."

Victoria set off obediently, consciously using her sticks.

"The family," she continued. "By that you mean Leonard and his son Maxim? Or are there other family members living in the hotel?"

"No, just the two of them."

"The first dead woman was Leonard's wife," Victoria said. "And Maxim was around twelve years old when she died, right?"

Karl nodded and became a little more talkative. "The poor boy hasn't coped well with his mother's death," he said, his voice sounding deeply sympathetic.

"Up until today, are you saying?" Victoria asked.

"He still hasn't really gotten over it, I think. He's not as depressed as he was in the early years, but he's still very introverted—a loner. He spends a lot of time in the forest instead of going out with other young people. He loves cross-country skiing, but not alpine skiing. There are too many people on the slopes for him, he says. But he's a good boy. Very intelligent ... and also helpful when you need him."

"You like him a lot," Victoria said.

Karl nodded. "Look ahead, not at your feet!"

Victoria jerked her head up.

"I'm worried about Maxim," Karl continued. "He hasn't had a single girlfriend yet, and he's already twenty. No real friends either, now that I think about it. But I think he likes Sissi, who is now Mr. Zauner's new girlfriend. Maybe too much."

He suddenly pressed his lips together. When he opened them again, he whispered: "No, I didn't say that."

"You mean he has a crush on her?" asked Victoria.

Karl nodded hesitantly, but then shrugged his strong shoulders. "Nothing wrong with it, I think, at his age. I had a crush on my teacher at school too. That's quite normal, isn't it? Or how do you see it as a psychologist?"

"I try to avoid talking about *normal* or *abnormal*," said Victoria. "But yes, in childhood and adolescence it's more common to have crushes on older people, and that's not a problem as long as it doesn't become an obsession. In your twenties—well, that's quite late, but it happens too."

Karl nodded in understanding. "Now let's concentrate on the trail, shall we?"

16

Pearl turned off the trail into the woods without warning. She didn't even seem to notice that she was brushing against thick branches and thorns and running through the mud.

"Where is Moonshadow?" she meowed. "Can't you find his trail, Athos?"

"I thought your nose was at least as good as mine?" I teased her.

However, she was in no mood for joking around.

"He's our most important witness!" she told me seriously. "We need him."

I stifled the half-dozen snide remarks that came to mind when I heard this claim.

The lynx *was* a valuable witness, or at least could become one if he kept his promise and made inquiries in the forest. But our most important one? So far, there was no question of that. Pearl had simply taken a fancy to the big cat.

How large was his territory, in which he roamed alone? His whole life without a pack—what a terrible thing to imagine.

My pack only consisted of one tiny cat and my two-leggeds, but that was more than enough. I had my paws full and couldn't really complain about boredom or loneliness.

When Moonshadow finally appeared, it was just like our first encounter: He was suddenly standing in front of us, under the branches of a majestic fir tree, without our having sniffed him out, heard him or noticed him in any other way. The cat was a true master of stalking, I had to give him that.

Pearl squealed with delight. And I ... didn't like that at all, I must admit, without being able to say why. I mean, it was okay for her to make other friends, apart from me. And after all, a lynx was also a cat, albeit a much bigger one, and therefore perhaps someone who could be closer to her than me.

Although that somehow seemed impossible—we knew each other so well by now that she could read my mind. I had saved her life countless times, and she had saved mine. And I could no longer picture a pack without the tiny one.

The lynx also seemed pleased to see us. Or should I say: to see Pearl? He greeted me in a friendly enough manner, but kept his distance.

"Two-leggeds have definitely been murdered in my territory," he told us without preamble. "I wandered around for a long time, and in more than one place the trees whispered of violence."

"So we're talking about murder," Pearl stated with the usual enthusiasm that this topic triggered in her. "And who is the culprit? Did the trees see him? Can you describe him to us?"

The lynx's brushed ears twitched. "Unfortunately, it doesn't work like that. I told you I cannot simply talk to the trees."

"They're just not as intelligent as we are, unfortunately, to understand us in detail," I said. "A pity—that would have been really helpful in this case."

Moonshadow fixed me with his amber-colored eyes, which shone conspicuously even in the semi-darkness of the forest.

"Not as intelligent?" he repeated. "That's exactly what the two-leggeds think of us, isn't it? That we're stupid, purely instinct-driven creatures who have neither a soul nor a real language."

"Right," I mumbled, ashamed.

I lifted my head and looked up the trunk of the large fir tree in whose shade we were standing.

"I'm sorry, tree," I said. "I really didn't mean to offend you or your kind."

Pearl puffed herself up a little. "Well, this information, that we're dealing with a murderer and not just accidental deaths, is very valuable. Just imagine if we had investigated this case with all our might only to find out in the end that the missing two-leggeds had just had a series of accidents. Or no longer wanted to live."

"I think you can rule that out," said Moonshadow.

"Good, good," said Pearl. "We—that is, our two-legged assistants, Tim and Victoria—have also already questioned some possible suspects among the humans. We've trained them very well to help us, you know."

"Really impressive," said Moonshadow.

Pearl looked as elated as if it were dinnertime. Freshly-caught salmon, *all you can eat*.

"And we already have a suspect," she continued.

"Oh, really?"

Moonshadow's voice was really pleasant: deep and warm and very calm. Although right now he sounded less peaceful and rather more obviously impressed by the criminalistic expertise Pearl was displaying.

"The hotelier knew all the missing two-leggeds intimately," Pearl explained. "They were all either his official partners or his secret mistresses, you know?"

Was it just my imagination, or did she wrinkle her nose in that very special way when she said those words—as she usually only did when she wanted to play the gentle, seductive kitten? Quite the opposite of the prickly beast I often had to deal with.

"It's really remarkable how you ... and Athos go about it, and what you find out," said the lynx. "I'm not generally particularly interested in the two-leggeds, but now I'm curious to see if you can solve this murder case. Oh, but I'm sure you will."

He scrutinized Pearl from head to tail and gave a soft but deep purr. He was clearly taking her much more seriously now than he had done when we first met.

"You could help us, Moonshadow," Pearl said. "With our investigation, that is. We could use someone to be our eyes and ears out here. We'd normally do that ourselves, but we're busy at the hotel."

And Pearl would start whining non-stop after half an hour out here in the cold, I thought to myself, but of course she didn't mention that.

"I'll be happy to help you, clever kitten," said the lynx. The look he was giving her grew even more intense.

"I'm not a kitten anymore," Pearl explained to him. "I only look like one because I have very special genes, you know—I'm actually a fully grown cat. In the prime of life, as they say."

She straightened her tail and arched her back. It wasn't the kind of hump you'd better avoid if you didn't want to get a scratched nose, but a gentler, much more elegant gesture. And suddenly Pearl smelled completely different, almost like Victoria when she kissed Tim. Although in a feline way, of course.

I was ... confused.

But then Moonshadow made a suggestion that caught my attention again.

"I can do more for you—for you both, so that you can solve this murder case," he said. "If those women you spoke of were murdered here in my forest, I will find their bodies."

"Oh, wow," Pearl purred. "That would be fantastic. Then people would realize that we really are dealing with a murderer—even the police. They have these forensic guys, you know, who can read all sorts of things from murder victims, even though people have such atrophied senses. They compensate for them with technical instruments and other stuff they've invented. Sometimes it's pretty impressive."

"All right, I'll go on a search," said Moonshadow. "You can count on me. We'll meet again, although it might take a while."

And with that, he left us in the way we were used to by now: silently, like a shadow blending into the semi-darkness between the trees.

"What a cat!" enthused Pearl on the way back to Victoria and her cross-country ski instructor. "He's so strong, Athos. And so graceful at the same time."

I refrained from commenting that I was also very strong—perhaps even stronger and more powerful than the lynx?

Hmm, maybe not. But his athletic appearance was mainly due to the fact that he had spent his whole life in the wild, where he had to find his own food and brave all kinds of weather, both things Pearl would never have even considered!

And graceful? Yes, you had to hand it to Moonshadow. Despite his size and visible musculature, he was incredibly light on his feet. I really wouldn't have wanted to be his prey. He certainly knew how to hunt with deadly precision, and yet he could also purr as softly as a big fluffy cuddly toy.

I wonder how suitable his front paws would be as a pil-

low, I suddenly thought.

I shook off the thought and walked a little faster.

Moonshadow could perhaps help us with our new case. That was what mattered. So far, he was our only four-pawed helper in this Killer's Wood, but he could fall back on other informants ... even if they were wearing bark and not fur. That was really a new thing for us. Our detective work always had surprises in store for me.

I had to think about what Moonshadow had said to me, that we animals underestimated trees just as much as humans did us. That we had far too little faith in the creatures clad in bark—and presumably all other plants, too—and hardly paid them the attention they deserved.

I let myself fall back a little without losing sight of Pearl. Finally, I halted.

I looked around until my gaze fell upon a slender young spruce tree that was growing by the side of the path and which looked somehow sociable.

I took a few steps towards it and gave it a friendly sniff, as I would have done with one of my own kind. I wagged my tail and panted a little. Then I tried to make polite conversation.

"You're a really handsome tree. How old are you? Do you like it here in this forest? Do you get enough light?"

I couldn't think of any more questions.

I became very still and tried to sense whether the tree was answering me. Perhaps it also had a question for me, too.

But no matter how much I listened and tried to empathize with it, I couldn't hear the slightest reaction. It seemed this kind of communication took a lot of practice and patience, as well as the necessary sensitivity.

I wondered how this young spruce conversed with the other trees growing nearby. What if it was surrounded by trees that were not its friends? It couldn't just run away; it was bound to this place. Forever. For centuries, perhaps....

Trees lived so much longer than we dogs did. Was that a blessing? A curse? Were these creatures happy within their bark skin? I had never thought about that before.

"Where are you, Athos?" I heard Pearl's voice. "What are you up to?"

"Nothing," I replied quickly. "I'm coming."

17

When we returned to the Alpenrose at the end of Victoria's cross-country skiing lesson, we met up with Alessio, the night porter.

We came across him in the hotel's ski room. He was obviously planning to set off on a cross-country trip of his own. I deduced this from his skis, which were long and narrow like Victoria's and not as wide as many of the other pairs standing around.

At first we didn't know who the man was, and Victoria only greeted him briefly—unaware that he was one of the witnesses we wanted to question.

He grabbed her hand and held it for far too long.

"How nice to meet you. Can you tell me your name? We seem to share a passion for Nordic skiing."

He pointed to her skis, which she was about to stow away in one of the wall brackets. "Oh please, let me do that for you," he offered eagerly.

Our human was a little surprised at the exuberant friendliness, but was happy to be assisted and introduced herself as Victoria Adler.

He stowed the skis away with two strong grips, then bowed with a playful gesture and told us who he was. "Alessio, night porter at the Alpenrose, the soul of the house, so to speak."

"Oh, excellent," said Victoria. "Your girlfriend recommended we talk to you."

"My girlfriend?"

"Tracy, the barmaid," Victoria clarified.

"Oh, her. Yes. And what did you want to talk to me about? How would you like me to show you the most beautiful cross-country skiing routes in the area? We'd have plenty of time to chat. Your little zoo is welcome to come along, of course."

He looked down at Pearl and me as if he had just realized that we were present as well.

"Very kind of you," Victoria said, "but I already have a tutor and I've just come back from a trip with him." She took a step backwards. Alessio had moved a little too close to her.

I sniffed him over and looked at him more closely. He spoke with the typical Tyrolean accent, which I liked and found kind of funny, but he looked like an Italian or a Spaniard: black hair, dark eyes, thick eyelashes and a full mouth with curved lips.

He wasn't particularly tall but had an athletic build, apart from a small belly. He smelled slightly of alcohol, which was unusual at this hour of the day, and had also used a very strong aftershave that stung my nose.

Why did the two-leggeds have such a problem with their body odor? Not only did they obsessively bathe and shower, some of them wrapped themselves in clouds of scent that took a dog's breath away. And a cat's too, I'm sure.

Whatever—what I actually want to say: I couldn't

claim that I took a liking to this night porter straight away.

"A tutor?" Alessio raised his eyebrows. "Not Karl, that bore? He radiates as much masculinity as a moth-eaten old hat, don't you think?"

Victoria frowned, but remained polite. "I'm not booking him for his manly charisma. I'm here with my boyfriend."

"Your boyfriend, huh?" Alessio said mockingly. "But you're still allowed to have a bit of fun, aren't you?" He casually stroked her arm.

She took another step back.

I growled softly—which at least dampened this slick player's thirst for action a little.

"I'm *having* fun, rest assured," said Victoria. "To be precise, a lot of fun—with Tim, my boyfriend. And you're dating Tracy, aren't you?"

"Did she say that?"

Victoria looked at him gravely. I gave her a gentle nudge with my muzzle to let her know that she could count on me. Alessio wouldn't dare become pushy ... I would make sure of that.

Her hand ran over my head. She scratched me a little behind the ears.

"I think Tracy is very much in love with you," she said to Alessio. "Even if I don't quite understand why," she added more quietly.

He didn't seem to hear her remark. "She's a nice little girl," he conceded, "and I have nothing against her.

Even if she is hopelessly romantic—and a bit uptight, to be honest."

Victoria frowned, but then finally came to her actual request. "You know, Alessio, my boyfriend and I are helping Henrik Engel look for his wife and sister-in-law, who disappeared from the hotel a week ago. I'm sure you've heard about it."

"Of course. Nothing that happens in the Alpenrose escapes me. I'm a very attentive observer."

"I'm glad to hear that. What can you tell me about the two women? Have you seen or heard anything that could help us find them? Or any clue as to who might be responsible for their disappearance?"

Alessio ran his tongue over his full lips. "What can you offer me in return if I'm willing to help you?"

"You want to be paid?" Victoria asked incredulously.

"Not at all, what do you think of me? But you could be a bit nicer." He tried to touch her arm again.

I'd had enough. This time I growled really viciously and bared my teeth.

I certainly don't want to show off, but my dentition is pretty impressive—and it didn't fail to make an impact this time either.

"Wow!" Alessio exclaimed. "That's a bit much! Your lapdog is quite hostile, my dear."

"He's just taking good care of me," Victoria countered. The look she gave me said: *Well done, Athos.*

She turned to Alessio: "Let's talk about it another time. You were just heading out to go cross-country skiing, weren't you? I don't want to keep you."

And with that she left the night porter standing there, looking quite bewildered.

18

Before dinner, Tim and Victoria met with Henrik in the library. It was supposed to be some kind of briefing, even though none of them seemed to have found out anything of interest.

Victoria mentioned that Alessio might be in possession of information, but that he didn't want to reveal it too easily.

"I think we need a little perseverance," she said to the two men, not mentioning how pushy the night porter had been towards her.

Then she added: "Perhaps we should have a chat with Maxim Zauner, the owner's son. He might—"

She didn't get any further, because at that moment Leonard Zauner appeared in the doorway.

"So here you are," he exclaimed. Instead of a greeting, a grim smile flitting across his face. It was feigned friendliness, but the scent that surrounded him told me that he was highly annoyed.

He was once again wearing a traditional outfit, and was clearly making an effort not to fall out of the role of the polite and always obliging hotelier, but tonight he seemed to be finding it very difficult to do so.

"Were you just talking about my son?" he asked.

Henrik was the first to react, and—once again—he was not particularly tactful.

"So what?" he snapped at Leonard. "Were you eavesdropping at the door? Is that your idea of good hospitality in your hotel?"

Leonard slammed the door behind him and then leaped towards us. He came to a halt in front of Henrik, who had been sitting in an armchair but who now jumped up. Tim also tensed his muscles in his wheelchair, albeit more reflexively, it seemed to me.

Was a growl indicated?

I decided against it. Victoria wasn't in any danger this time; neither was Tim. And the atmosphere in the room already seemed heated enough to me.

Leonard was visibly struggling to keep calm. He stood stock-still, legs apart, and I saw him take a few deep breaths in and out.

Then he said: "I've heard that you're putting my staff through the wringer—yes, even my girlfriend! I must protest against this in the strongest possible terms. You are guests in my hotel and I can understand that you, Mr. Engel, are going through a very difficult time at the moment. But that certainly doesn't give you the right to behave like the worst kind of snoop. Have you asked yourself what effect this might have on my other guests? Your behavior is damaging to my business! And under no circumstances will I allow you to frighten my girlfriend!"

"It seems to me that being your girlfriend is a pretty dangerous occupation," Henrik interjected. "Dear Sissi should probably be more afraid of you than of us."

This was the end of Leonard's self-control.

"How dare you talk to me like that!" he exclaimed, his face darkening. "You'd better put your own house in order, you damn hypocrite!"

Victoria now jumped up from the sofa too.

"Please, gentlemen, let's all keep calm, shall we? It won't get us anywhere if we're at each other's throats. We need to concentrate on Natalia and Fabienne. Their lives may be in danger while we're here..."

"If they're not dead by now!" Leonard interrupted her. "And maybe you should ask this man about that, who is making himself seem so important as a crime expert, instead of pestering me and my staff!"

He jabbed his index finger into Henrik's chest as if he wanted to stab him with it. Fortunately, the two-leggeds don't have any claws worth mentioning on their fingers, otherwise blood would have been flowing by now.

"What are you trying to say?" Tim interposed, grabbing Henrik's arm at the same time. Otherwise, Henrik's fist would probably have flown into Leonard's face.

Leonard laughed diabolically. "Yes, that makes you listen up, doesn't it? I'm telling you, this fine gentleman here, who is acting like such an eager investigator, may have a skeleton in the closet himself—or rather, two! He cheated on his wife, did you know? With her own sister! Well, no, to be precise: he *tried to* cheat on her. He was constantly hitting on his sister-in-law and wasn't even attempting to be discreet about it. Half my staff noticed it."

A snide grin twitched at the corners of his mouth. "I don't think she fell for him, so she's not to blame. Instead, she revealed to her sister how inappropriately Mr. Engel was behaving, and then the couple had a heated argument about it."

Although Tim only had one hand at his disposal, and was not in a good position to keep Henrik under control from the wheelchair, he somehow managed to maneuver the man back into his armchair. There he sat literally foaming at the mouth, but surprisingly did not protest against the hotelier's claims.

"Apparently what Leonard says is true," Pearl concluded.

"The fact that Henrik fancied Natalia is nothing new to us," I said.

"Yes, but that his wife knew about it—and that it was why they had their heated argument—he's kept that from us until now."

Pearl was right.

Leonard wasn't finished yet, however. He now completely ignored Henrik and addressed his words to Tim and Victoria only. "Don't think that I'm into eavesdropping on my guests—I only overheard the argument because I happened to be nearby and the three of them got really loud. But it goes even further back in time, because the day before the argument, my Sissi witnessed a conversation that took place here in the library, between the two sisters. And Fabienne said something quite unbelievable to Natalia."

"It seems to me that the walls are really thin in this hotel," I said, turning to Pearl. "Or Leonard and his staff are *really* interested in their guests' affairs."

"My thoughts exactly," said the tiny one. "But in this case, that works in our favor."

"Go on," Tim said to the hotelier, while continuing to ensure that Henrik didn't lose his temper.

But Henrik was now sitting in his armchair like an old man with his head in his hands. Was he overcome with remorse?

Or was he just pretending in order to deceive us, because he suddenly looked like a suspect himself? If he had been unfaithful, or at least tried to be, and had chosen his own sister-in-law of all people to get involved with, then perhaps his wife had had enough of him. Perhaps the two of them not only argued violently, but she also threatened him with divorce.

But could that be a reason to kill her? And her sister too?

Leonard didn't need to be asked twice to elaborate. "Well, in the conversation that Sissi overheard, Natalia said to Fabienne, in plain words: 'I've tried to ignore his chat-up lines for so long, but the truth is that he made eyes at me from when he first met you.'"

"And she didn't tell her sister that back then?" Victoria asked.

"Obviously not," said Leonard. "Fabienne asked her exactly that question—why she had kept quiet for so long. And her answer was: 'Because you were so in love with him and seemed so happy.'"

"Wow," said Tim, "that may have been well-intentioned, but it was a stupid idea to hide something like that for so long."

"I agree," said Leonard. "But here's the thing: During the argument between the spouses the next day—the one I overheard—Fabienne said to her husband: 'When I met you, we talked about *Lolita* once. I still remember that. The book by Vladimir Nabokov in which a man marries a woman, not out of love for her, but because he is actually infatuated with her daughter. He only enters into the marriage to be close to the girl. And you did the same to me, you disgusting bastard! I realize that now. Maybe you even got the idea from the novel, but anyway, you married me just to be close to Natalia. Admit it!'"

"And he did?" Tim asked breathlessly.

Henrik jumped out of his armchair as if bitten by a snake.

I reacted on instinct, without thinking. I leaped up, threw myself at him and dragged him to the ground.

"Help!" he shouted. "Call off your dog!"

Within moments, his raging anger had turned to fear for his life. "I didn't mean to hurt anyone I swear," he stammered.

Victoria suddenly stood over me and pulled on my collar. "Good boy, Athos. Let go of the man now."

I obeyed.

Pearl appeared next to me and said: "What a big leap. And well deserved in his case."

The pugnacious expression on the tiny one's face—and her compliment—cheered me up a little.

Henrik pulled himself up and returned to his armchair, feeling his bones as if I had hurt him badly. Which wasn't the case, of course. The most he could have suffered was a few bruises.

There was a short pause, during which the four people were embarrassedly silent, then Henrik raised his head and jutted out his chin.

"Yes, I love Natalia; I won't deny it any longer. And it's true that Nabokov's book gave me the idea of marrying Fabienne, but not because I was planning to cheat on her from the start. I liked her, and I just wanted to be close to Natalia. I knew I didn't stand a chance with her. She was so clever, so beautiful..."

"You already said that," Tim mumbled.

"But she just didn't take notice of me, didn't see me as a man at all, and that gnawed at me. So at some point I did start chasing her. I wanted her to at least notice how I felt about her, to make her see how much I wanted her..."

He broke off again and a deep, agonized sigh escaped his chest. "I was such a fool. And now I may have lost them both. I loved Fabienne, too. Not the same as I did Natalia. But I did!"

19

Leonard Zauner turned to leave, but as he opened the door to walk out of the library, a hotel guest was standing there, flinching away from him, startled.

Had he been listening at the door? I was getting the impression that this was the favorite pastime of the humans in this place.

The man was Richard Schöndorf.

"Oh, hello," he exclaimed sheepishly as Leonard almost collided with him. "I just ... wanted to borrow some new reading material. May I?"

He pushed past Leonard into the room, and the latter now moved out the door as he'd intended. The look he gave Richard before he disappeared, however, spoke volumes. It was obvious to everyone that the man must have been eavesdropping.

I wondered how much he had overheard. The ears of the two-leggeds aren't the best, but on the other hand, the men in the room had gotten quite loud at the end of their argument.

Richard stood there for a moment, embarrassed, staring at the bookshelves. But then he seemed to decide to give up his obvious pretext and walked towards my two-leggeds with his hand outstretched.

"Richard Schöndorf," he introduced himself. "I witnessed your argument with Mr. Zauner quite by chance."

"Quite by chance, I'm sure," Henrik grumbled, but then deigned to shake the hand that Richard held out to him. "Henrik Engel," he said, "but I assume you already know that."

Tim and Victoria also introduced themselves, and Pearl and I assumed that Richard would come out to them as a die-hard true crime fan.

But he didn't do that. Instead, he said something unexpected: "I think I can come clean with you. I'm not in the hotel to ski or to relax. I'm the brother of Beate Krüger, who disappeared from the Alpenrose six months ago. She worked here as a barmaid at the hotel until one day she didn't return from a trip into the forest. The police searched for her, but soon closed the case. So officially she's still missing, but they're not really doing anything to find her anymore. But *I'm* not going to give up. I will find her, dead or alive. And if I get my hands on the guy who did this to her..."

His hands clenched into fists, although he had spoken in a very controlled whisper. He probably knew only too well by now that the library door was not very soundproof and had no desire to be overheard by anyone himself.

Henrik's mouth hung wide open. He tried to say something, but only an unintelligible mumble escaped his lips.

Richard put a hand on his shoulder. "I know how you must feel. I overheard that Zauner guy telling you off.

You messed up, man, there's no question about it. To betray your own wife like that—"

Henrik found his voice again, even if it sounded rather hoarse. "Yes, thank you, I really need a sermon from you as well!"

Richard shrugged his shoulders. "Zauner was perhaps just trying to deflect attention from himself by attacking you; didn't that thought occur to you? He's anything but a saint, you know."

Henrik straightened his shoulders. If he had been a four-legged with flexible ears, he would certainly have turned them fully towards Richard by now.

"What do you know? Let's hear it!" he demanded.

Richard didn't have to be asked twice. He took a seat in one of the two armchairs that were still free, then said: "So then, our esteemed host is a real ladies' man, there's no other way to put it. And from what I've already found out about him, he doesn't care who he chooses. Guests, whether single or married, and the hotel's female staff too, of course."

Henrik nodded impatiently. "Yes, we already know that."

An arrogant expression appeared on Richard's face. "But what you probably don't know yet is: He has very strange preferences ... in the bedroom, that is. Beate told me that during one of our phone calls just before she disappeared. And unfortunately, she was so naive that she thought that kind of stuff was hot. Women are reading all this garbage these days—bondage games, whippings, submission, even torture—it's all in these trashy novels they love to devour. They worship perverts like Leonard Zauner instead of running away screaming. Beate was completely in thrall to that creep, you see."

Henrik stared at the man with wide eyes. Apparently, he hadn't known about *this*, just as Richard had predicted. Neither had Pearl and I, of course.

"Zauner had my sister in his power," Richard continued.

By now he was no longer whispering, but had pretty much worked himself into a rage. Beads of sweat glistened on his forehead.

"This man is a psychopath, a sexual predator! I bet he murdered my poor Beate. Perhaps at some point she no longer wanted to play along with his violent fantasies. Unfortunately, she didn't confide in me, but I'm sure that's how it must have gone. And then this lecher got rid of her—just like he did with all the other women who have disappeared from this hotel!"

"But the police have assumed that the women who didn't go missing but who were found dead in the forest over the years must have suffered accidents," Victoria objected. "If sexual violence had been involved, surely they would have found evidence of it."

Richard snorted contemptuously. "Psychopaths like Zauner know how to torture without leaving a trace. Well, no visible traces, I should say. Nobody can see the psychological injuries he may have inflicted on my sister, and who knows how many other women."

"You seem to be quite familiar with this kind of stuff," Tim remarked.

Richard ignored the interruption. Instead, he stared at Henrik expectantly. "We have to do something, man! We can't count on the police. And maybe at least your two women can still be saved, if not my poor sister."

The way he said it made me think of a harem, but Henrik didn't seem to have a problem with the wording.

Henrik and our two-leggeds continued their conversation with Richard Schöndorf for a while after dinner. It seemed they had accepted him as another member of their investigation team—and now the four amateur sleuths openly exchanged the information they had gathered thus far.

Pearl commented: "I really fear that Leonard's new girlfriend, Sissi, could also be in danger. Even though he's apparently so worried about her safety—it could all be an act. Maybe he's one of those monsters who are harmless most of the time, only to turn into werewolves or something similar on some nights."

Once again, Tiny was letting her imagination run wild.

"I'm not convinced that werewolves really exist," I remarked.

In the past, I would have insisted that these creatures were pure invention, but after all Pearl and I had been through, I wouldn't have placed any bets on it. We had encountered some very strange beings during our murder cases, and who could have said what else walked our earth at night, in the dark....

"It's almost a full moon," Pearl said to snap me out of my thoughts.

I had no better reply than that we really needed to keep an eye on Sissi, which was easier said than done. After all, we couldn't be at her side 24/7 to protect her. And then there was a number of other women in the hotel who might also be in danger.

I suddenly felt somehow small and helpless. How could we make sure that someone else from this hotel in the middle of this enormous forest wouldn't lose their life?

It was the middle of the night when I was suddenly startled out of my sleep.

I couldn't tell if I had been tormented by a nightmare, but somehow it felt like it. I had awoken with a pounding heart and looked around anxiously for Pearl. She wasn't lying on my paw.

I got to my feet and ran over to the bed. But up on the mattress I only saw Tim and Victoria, both breathing peacefully. Pearl wasn't lying on top of them or between them, as she liked to do from time to time.

I finally found her sitting upright in front of the glass patio door. She was sitting motionless behind the lowest pane, staring out into the night.

I trotted over to her and touched her with my muzzle. "Tiny? Are you all right? What are you doing here? Can't you sleep?"

She flinched—but I really hadn't sneaked up on her.

"It's just me," I whispered.

She raised her head and looked at me with concern in her baby-blue eyes.

"Look how heavy the rain is," she said to me. "And I bet it's freezing cold too."

"But we're in here in the warmth," I replied. "Are you cold? I could warm you up a bit if you like."

"Poor Moonshadow is all alone out there!" she moaned. She narrowed her eyes and stared even more intently into the darkness. "In the pouring rain, you know."

Goodness gracious.

"I'm sure he has a dry shelter," I assured her, "although I don't think rain or cold would bother a forest dweller like him. They can't harm me either when I'm out roaming around, and I'm a house wolf after all. While Moonshadow has lived in this forest all his life."

"His beautiful fur will get all wet and dirty!" complained Pearl.

I really didn't know what to say to that. But I tried: "Well, his fur looks very silky, don't you think? I noticed that when we first met him. So he will have found a way to take care of it, even in bad weather."

"Yes, that's right, it does look very silky." Pearl's voice

suddenly took on a dreamy, rapturous tone.

The next moment, however, her face grew worried again. "But he'll still freeze," she said. "Look, even the water is already freezing—icicles are hanging from the trees. Shouldn't we get Moonshadow in here with us?"

"*Get him in*?" I repeated incredulously. "Into the hotel? Are you crazy? Tim and Victoria would have a heart attack if they found a fully-grown lynx in their room."

"Do you really think so?"

"Of course! They would probably be very scared of him themselves, but above all they would be worried about you, that the lynx might do something to you. You fit right into his prey pattern—in terms of size."

"Moonshadow would never hurt me," Pearl protested. "He's *nice*."

"Yes, of course he is," I said quickly. "But Victoria and Tim don't know that."

"And he likes me."

"Please, Tiny, come to your senses! We really can't bring him to the hotel. But we'll check on him again first thing tomorrow, okay? And I promise you he'll be fine. He's, um, a very big and strong cat. That's what you said. He's honestly quite good at looking after himself."

I finally managed to convince Pearl.

"Shall we go back to sleep?" I suggested. "I'm sure we'll have our paws full again tomorrow and hardly have time for a siesta."

"Hmm, I'm really not tired," she mumbled. And then

she continued to stare out into the night.

I stayed sitting next to her for a while until I finally trotted over to Victoria and curled up on the rug.

20

When we set off on our morning walk the next day, an enchanted winter wonderland awaited us. The rain must have turned to snowfall at some point during the last few hours of the night, and the whole landscape was now a sparkling white in the light of the morning sun.

Pearl immediately turned off into the undergrowth and ran to the clearing where we had first met Moonshadow.

"Don't stay too long," Victoria called after us. Fortunately, she always gave us plenty of space to roam on our walks, but it was really bitterly cold that morning so her patience would certainly be limited.

Pearl didn't complain once about the freezing temperatures, but sniffed around on the ground, stared into the copse and finally called Moonshadow's name.

The lynx, however, did not show up.

"Where might he be, Athos?" she meowed in worry.

I couldn't sniff out any trace of the big cat either, but that didn't surprise me. We knew by now that he could only be found if he wanted to be.

"Maybe he's sleeping," I suggested. "Lynxes are mainly nocturnal, I think. And his territory must be huge. Why would he hang out near the hotel?"

For my sake, I heard Pearl thinking. Or was I just imagining it?

I wanted to say more to reassure her, but suddenly the smell of a human caught my nose. I turned my head and walked a few steps in the direction it had come from.

Yes, definitely a human. And it had to be someone I'd met before, because the smell seemed somehow familiar.

Pearl now also pressed her nose to the earth. However, just like me, she had difficulties in assigning the smell to the right person.

We followed the trail. It led deeper into the forest.

We hadn't walked far when I suddenly heard a soft moan. Or maybe it was a loud moan, but from some distance away. Pearl and I quickened our steps.

I trotted along, she broke into a gallop. As always, I adapted my pace to hers, because there was no way I was going to let her out of my sight here in the forest. Moonshadow might not be out to eat her, but there were certainly plenty of other forest dwellers who would have had no qualms about it.

Pearl stopped abruptly. "Wait a minute. Do you hear that?"

I slowed down and listened. "Footsteps. Someone is running. And pretty fast?"

Was there a human on the run?

"Come on, Tiny, full throttle!" I exclaimed, and I didn't have to tell her twice. When she wasn't playing the spoiled and lazy sofa cat, Pearl could run amazingly fast.

The moaning was getting louder now and the footsteps could be heard quite clearly. That is, it wasn't actually a moan, but rather a panting sound. It sounded as if one of my own kind had been transported straight into the heat of the tropics.

I turned right, always listening for the sounds. Pearl followed at my heels, and soon the undergrowth cleared and we reached a narrow path.

A woman was running ahead of us.

Sissi! Now that I saw her in front of me, I could also identify the smell I had detected. It was a floral scent with a hint of vanilla, but also unmistakable undertones of tobacco.

I barked to draw attention to Pearl and me—whereupon Sissi promptly stopped and whirled around.

"Oh, it's you two. You gave me quite a fright!"

She came up to us, got down on her knees and scratched Pearl's head. "Are you wandering around here all alone? Where's your mistress?"

"She wasn't on the run at all," commented the tiny one. "She was just jogging."

Pearl was right: Sissi was wearing running clothes, had her long blonde hair tied back in a tight ponytail, and pink sneakers on her feet. She was still actually panting. Apparently she had pushed herself hard while running. The pace she had set had been remarkable—

otherwise Pearl and I would hardly have thought of someone running for their life.

Just as I was relaxing because, for once, we didn't have to come to anyone's rescue, I heard footsteps again.

A second person was out and about in the forest. He was approaching on a path that crossed ours a few meters away, and before I could draw Pearl's attention to him, he was already in front of us—maybe fifteen or twenty meters away.

"Leonard? What are you doing here?" Sissi gasped.

"He's holding something, Athos!" Pearl hissed at me. "A knife?"

I squinted my eyes. We were surrounded by twilight. In some places it was actually pitch black, but where the rays of sunlight fell through the treetops we were almost blinded. I found it difficult to make out exactly what the man was holding. His fingers were clutching it and his hand was half hidden in the sleeve of his jacket.

"I think it's a knife," Pearl exclaimed excitedly. "Look how the tip sparkles."

She was right; I could see the telltale glitter too.

Leonard came running up to Sissi—which didn't seem to scare her. She even spread her arms and exclaimed: "What a surprise, my darling. It's good to see you!"

His rapid approach, on the other hand, made the fur on the back of my neck stand on end. Was he really carrying a knife in his hand? If so, he had to have sinister intentions. No one takes an instrument of murder with them on an innocent walk in the woods.

"We have to stop him, Athos!" meowed Pearl. "Look how tense he looks! We can't wait for another disaster to happen."

I knew exactly what she was alluding to: In our last murder case, we had hesitated too long before intervening, which had almost cost a young woman her life.

I wouldn't make a mistake like that a second time.

I boldly charged straight towards the hotelier, who was only a few meters away from us. I swung to the right because he was holding the knife in his right hand and I didn't want to run straight into the blade, but I wasn't really afraid of it. It wasn't a huge instrument, otherwise he wouldn't have been able to conceal it in his hand, and I'd had encounters with far more terrifying weapons in the past.

I leapt and threw myself at him from the side. He cursed and lost his balance—and the weapon slipped from his fingers. A cylindrical instrument landed on the forest floor.

It wasn't a knife.

It had a sharp, shiny silver tip—what Pearl and I had assumed to be a blade—but the rest was matt gray and somehow reminded me of a ballpoint pen.

What the hell...?

After Leonard landed on the forest floor, I didn't pin him down as I had intended. Instead, I stood there, quite perplexed, staring at the strange pen.

Sissi scolded me. "Get away from him, you crazy mutt! Oh, my poor Leonard, did he hurt you?"

She ran to her boyfriend and helped him to his feet while glaring at me.

I took a few steps to the side. I hadn't exactly expected gratitude, but that was pretty mean.

But then Sissi also spotted the strange pen that Leonard had dropped. She let go of his arm, bent down and picked it up.

"What's this?" she asked.

Leonard took the thing from her. "Uh, it's a tactical pen. You can write with it, but the tip is reinforced so that you can defend yourself if necessary. And it's small and inconspicuous enough that you can always have it with you."

"But what for...?" Sissi stared at him uncomprehendingly, whereupon he suddenly became angry.

"You're still asking me that? After I practically begged you not to go into the forest alone while this woman-killer is on the loose? And what are you doing—you're jogging along as if you couldn't care less. That's why I followed you ... and armed myself. This thing gives you an advantage in a fight. Unless you get shot, that is; but this forest-murderer here hasn't used any firearms, at least not yet. Someone would inevitably have heard that."

"Are we going to accept this explanation from him, Athos?" Pearl commented impatiently. "Or do you think it's all just an excuse? Did he try to kill Sissi or not?"

"We probably won't find out now," I said.

"We should have waited to see if he actually was going to attack her," said Pearl.

"And risk her dying?" I objected. "We agreed..."

"Yes, yes, but he could hardly have seriously injured her with this thing."

"Except that we didn't see exactly what he was holding," I reminded her. Did she really have to criticize me now, after Sissi had already treated me so unkindly?

Pearl seemed to sense my frustration. She stuck out her tiny pink tongue and licked my muzzle. "It's all right. That was a really great leap, Athos."

"Thank you," I mumbled, already half reconciled. You really couldn't stay angry with the tiny one for long.

Sissi snuggled into Leonard's arms. "How sweet that you care so much about me. That you came to save me..."

"What do you think?" said Leonard. "I don't want anything to happen to you." He kissed her on the forehead, but his eyes wandered left and right—as if he expected an attack at any moment.

"If he's our killer, he's really good at pretending to be fearful," I said to Pearl.

"Mm-hmm, that's true."

"Come on, let's go back to the hotel," Leonard suggested to his sweetheart. "And could you *please* use the gym from now on? Just until the disappearance of those two women is solved?"

"Who's going to solve it?" Sissi replied. "Those pathetic amateur sleuths? I'd probably have to hide in the hotel for all eternity."

Leonard groaned. "Then I'll go with you from now on if you want to go jogging. Okay? A bit of exercise won't do me any harm."

He grinned wryly, holding up the pen he still had in his hand. "My sword and I are yours to command, my lady!"

She threw herself into his arms again and kissed him passionately. "My hero!" she purred.

"Crap," Pearl commented. "If he accompanies her from now on, he'll have an opportunity to murder her every time. In case he is our killer after all."

"And we can't always be around to protect her," I said.

Pearl wrinkled her nose. "Moonshadow could watch out..."

She stared into the semi-darkness of the forest, much like Leonard had just done. Her gaze slid from tree to tree, over frost-glistening branches and bushes, and over the white patches of snow in between. But there was still no sign of the lynx.

"I think Moonshadow really has better things to do than devote himself to people-sitting," I tried to comfort her.

Pearl looked over at me seriously. "Yes, that's certainly true. As Lord of the Forest, he must be very busy." Her voice took on an almost reverent tone.

"Lord of the Forest?" I repeated. "Now you're exaggerating."

"Who could compete with him in that role? Such a proud and powerful cat?"

A wolf? was on the tip of my tongue, but I stifled the remark.

A whole pack of wolves perhaps?

My wild counterparts had become rare in the forests of Central Europe, but as far as I knew there were still a few scattered populations. There was always talk of it on television; indeed, some countries were even trying to actively reintroduce the wolf.

However, I had never met one yet.

Maybe I just needed to search more thoroughly for my free-living cousins. If Pearl had made friends with this lynx, then maybe I could meet a pretty, wild she-wolf. With silver fur and ice blue eyes?

No ... the color of her fur and eyes didn't matter at all.

21

"Do you hear that?" Pearl suddenly snapped me out of my trance.

"Hmm?" I asked, half-absentmindedly.

"Someone's coming! Moonshadow maybe?" Her tone sounded hopeful. That must have been why she couldn't seem to think straight.

"Moonshadow would never make a racket like that," I said. I heard the sound approaching us now too. "That's a two-legged. For sure."

We both set off and bravely pushed our way through the undergrowth. That is, Pearl had no trouble gliding through, while I was once again grateful for my thick fur that protected me from sharp twigs and thorns. Snow trickled down on me from the tree branches, but that felt wonderful.

The smell of a human caught my nose and confirmed my suspicions—and I had no difficulty finding him. Behind a bush, which currently had no leaves but plenty of branches, I came across a young man.

I barked to draw Leonard and Sissi's attention to him. Who was he? Not the murderer we were looking for? We couldn't possibly be that lucky!

I had never seen him before, that much was certain. He had not long outgrown his childhood years, possessed a handsome face and shoulder-length, very curly brown hair, and he had been hiding behind this bush. Had he been following Sissi for a long time? Would he have pounced on her if Leonard hadn't shown up?

I barked a little louder and growled at him.

However, he wasn't the least bit afraid, just angry. Like Sissi before him, he insulted me and then left his hiding place without me having to push him out. He fought his way through the dense bushes and trees, closely followed by Pearl and me, until he reached the forest path where we had left Leonard and Sissi.

"Maxim?" Leonard gasped. "Where did you come from? What on earth are you doing here?"

"His son," I hissed at Pearl, but she had already figured it out for herself.

"Leonard doesn't seem too pleased to see him," she commented.

And she was right. Sissi greeted the young man in a friendly manner, while Leonard pursed his lips and repeated his question in a serious, or even hostile, tone of voice: "What are you doing here, boy?"

"I could ask you the same thing," Maxim replied. His voice sounded brighter than his father's, but he seemed just as suspicious as the older two-legged.

"I don't think I owe you an account of my activities," said Leonard.

Sissi, however, touched his arm and smiled conciliatorily. She said to Maxim: "Your father is accompanying me. Just for protection, because here in the forest ... oh, you know."

"Because women keep disappearing here?" Maxim replied. "Yes, I do indeed know that."

Did it just seem that way to me, or was he glaring at his father with even more hostility?

Maxim scrutinized Sissi. His gaze wandered over her face, then over her body. "Is everything all right with you? Are you okay?" he asked in a much friendlier tone.

"Oh yes," she said lightly. She hooked herself up with Leonard on the right and Maxim on the left.

"Shall we go home, my dear boys? Are you also longing for a nice hot cup of coffee?"

I wanted to let the three of them go and return to our own two-legged, who must have missed us already.

But Pearl said: "Victoria should know that these three have come together here, I think. Whatever that means—I can't really make heads or tails of it."

"All right," I said and started yapping so loudly that you could probably hear it all the way to the hotel. Victoria had certainly not ventured far from there on her walk, and if she heard my voice, she would probably make her way in my direction and then see Sissi and the two men.

Hopefully my poor human wasn't half frozen to death by now, I thought.

But then an even more terrible thought occurred to me: I had left Victoria alone! Completely defenseless in this forest where a murderer of women was on the loose. What had I been thinking?

Nothing at all, was the honest answer. It hadn't even

occurred to me that she could be in danger.

I had to be more careful in future. More responsible. I had to protect my pack, not just potential murder victims like Sissi Fassbender.

I didn't have to yelp for long before I heard Victoria's voice calling out to me: "Athos? Where are you?"

"They're here with us," Leonard answered her aloud, and he shouted more directions to Victoria until she finally joined us.

I greeted her ruefully for having neglected her so much, but then yelped again, circling Sissi and the two men to let Victoria know that this meeting of the three two-leggeds here in the forest was perhaps significant. Although, to be honest, I couldn't really make sense of it. Who had actually been following whom, and above all, for what motive?

22

When we got back to the hotel, Richard Schöndorf and Henrik Engel were standing in front of the building, whispering and putting their heads together conspiratorially.

Richard was smoking a cigarette, and Henrik was apparently keeping him company, although he wasn't smoking himself. Neither of them was wearing a jacket or coat, but they were talking so animatedly that they didn't even seem to notice the cold.

Leonard, Maxim and Sissi greeted them in passing, but didn't stop, instead disappearing into the hotel.

Victoria, on the other hand, joined the two men, whereupon they suddenly fell silent. They smelled very excited, as if they had just been discussing something particularly interesting or making bold plans.

Victoria was probably getting a similar impression as I was—even if she wasn't as blessed in the nasal department. "Is there any news?" she asked.

But both men shook their heads almost simultaneously. "Not really. With you, Victoria? What were you doing with the hoteliers in the forest?"

"I only met them by chance. Athos and Pearl were with them." Victoria suddenly looked thoughtful and glanced down at me. Was she wondering if the tiny one and I had run to those two-leggeds for a reason?

I would have liked to tell her what Pearl and I had observed, even though I couldn't really make sense of it. But that was impossible in any case.

"Let's go inside," said Henrik, "before we freeze to death out here." His eyes searched meaningfully for Richard's—behind Victoria's back. Unfortunately, I couldn't tell her that either.

In the afternoon, Victoria had another training session with Karl. By now, she was doing quite well on the miserably long footboards and only rarely fell on her nose.

She also took the opportunity to question Karl further about the missing women. First, she asked about Beate Krüger, Richard's sister, who had been a barmaid at the Alpenrose and had been missing for six months.

When Victoria casually remarked: "I've heard that Beate was close friends with Leonard Zauner," Karl didn't seem surprised.

"Maybe," he said, shrugging his shoulders. "Leonard is ... how do you say it? Not a prisoner of grief. He didn't remarry after his wife died, but even so he probably tries to have a bit of fun now and again. Kind of understandable, isn't it? As far as I know, he's been with some of his female employees. Sometimes only for a fairly short time. But he was always quite discreet about it."

"And he was also friends with female guests at the hotel from time to time?" asked Victoria.

"Yes, that did happen—but why do you care? You

don't suspect him, do you? As a ... murderer?"

"Would you rule him out one hundred percent as a possible culprit, Karl?

The ski instructor thought about it for a moment. He nodded.

"Yes, I would. Leonard is all right. As I said, not a prisoner of grief nor even a saint, but each of us has a little vice and one or two idiosyncrasies. He's certainly not a murderer. If you think that, you're barking up the wrong tree."

Victoria lost her balance and let out a small scream. However, Karl deftly grabbed her by the arm, as he had done so many times before, before she could fall. The man had excellent reflexes.

"You need to concentrate on the trail, my dear Miss Marple," he joked.

She grinned sheepishly, but didn't miss the opportunity to probe a little further. "Leonard seems to have found just the right partner in Sissi. It's more than just a flirtation, isn't it?"

Karl's eyes narrowed.

I thought he wasn't going to answer, but after a soft groan that faded into the winter sky as a small white cloud would, he did. "Yes, they're a dream couple, so to speak. It's a wonder they only got together now."

"Why is that?" asked Victoria.

She started to look rather embarrassed. She didn't like grilling people and having to be so persistent, but Karl wasn't the kind to talk and talk voluntarily without wanting to stop. You had to draw the information out of him like pulling teeth.

"Sissi has been working at the hotel for a very long time," he said. "But she's really blossomed in the last few years. Mentally, physically—and also in terms of her looks. While others are getting older, she's somehow getting fitter, more educated and more attractive. Really impressive! I can understand why Leonard is crazy about her."

"And you as well, Karl?" Victoria said with a laugh. She almost lost her balance again.

I felt really sorry for my poor human. Being out and about without the right balance and having to carry out a rather tough interrogation while struggling to keep on your feet was certainly not easy. I would have liked to help her, but when it came to eliciting specific information from two-leggeds, my hands were simply tied—or should I say, my paws.

Karl was laughing now too.

"What, me? No, Sissi's not my type! She's a good ten years older than me. Not that I have anything against more mature women," he added, suddenly looking embarrassed. "Like I said, I just find it impressive how Sissi has transformed herself. From shy ugly duckling to radiant swan, you could say. And you have to admire that—it proves that you can achieve almost anything if you work on yourself consistently. Now let's get back to practicing, shall we?"

Victoria nodded obediently. She seemed glad that she

had brought her little interrogation session to a close.

Pearl and I turned into the forest. Without her having to mention it, I knew she was looking for Moonshadow.

After we had been sniffing and looking around for a while, the tiny one started to whine.

"Still no sign of him. Where could he be? Surely nothing has happened to him?"

She looked so worried that you could actually feel sorry for her.

"The Lord of the Forest? What could possibly have happened to him?" I replied a little snippily. I didn't know why, because I really had nothing against the lynx. And he'd helped us with the investigation; there was no denying that.

But in my humble opinion, Pearl was a little too infatuated with him.

23

In the evening, Victoria and Tim went together to see Alessio. They had to wait until he started his shift, because they hadn't been able to track him down before. And then we had to be patient yet again because he had to deal with some hotel guests who had come to reception with questions or requests.

But finally we were alone with him.

"We'd like to talk to you again, Alessio," Victoria began the conversation. "We are trying to do everything we can to perhaps save the lives of Mr. Engel's wife and sister-in-law. So I would like to ask you: If you have any information that can help us, please let us know." She particularly emphasized the word *us,* as if Tim's presence alone wasn't a clear signal that she hadn't come to flirt.

Alessio scrutinized her closely before answering. At least now that Tim was here, he held back with his insinuating remarks, but that didn't make him friendly and courteous.

"Really touching, my dear. You are a true altruist," he replied flippantly. "But there has to be a little incentive if you want me to do something for you. What's the saying? You get what you pay for."

Victoria wanted to say something in reply, but Tim gently placed his uninjured hand on her arm. Then he pulled his wallet out of his inside jacket pocket. He took out a green banknote and placed it on the reception counter in front of Alessio.

The night porter clicked his tongue. "Are you trying to insult me, man?"

Tim added another bill.

"That's better." Alessio suddenly grinned. "But to use another nice saying: All good things come in threes."

Victoria tried to protest, but Tim just shook his head. Which probably meant something like: It's not worth negotiating with a guy like this.

Alessio took the three bills and slipped them into his jacket.

I was now really curious to hear what he had to say. Would we find out more things about Leonard that would put the hotel owner in a bad light?

Not at all, as it turned out.

Because Alessio immediately began to talk about *Henrik*. "You said that you wanted to help this guy find his women—his wife and sister-in-law, I mean. Although, that wording isn't completely wrong, because he clearly wanted them both. This sister-in-law was also a hottie, I tell you. A man who wasn't tempted by her would have to be a priest!"

"We've already heard about all of that," said Tim. "Mr. Engel even admitted it himself. And also that Natalia and Fabienne left him after an argument, although he would have liked to keep quiet about what the argument entailed."

"I'm not surprised he didn't want to come out with it. None of us would have been keen to do that, would we?" Alessio grinned as if he was having the time of his life. "But I'm not talking about the argument the three of them might have had during the day. I didn't hear anything about that."

"But what, then?" asked Victoria.

"Well, put two and two together, my dear! I'm the night porter here—I sleep during the day. But on my night shifts, I'm also responsible for that little bar right here after midnight."

He pointed to the counter that adjoined the reception. In front of it were two high chairs, and behind it were shelves lined with bottles and glasses.

"The bar beside the restaurant closes at twelve, as you may have noticed, and anyone who is still thirsty after that comes to me, do you understand? We don't leave our guests high and dry."

"And Henrik was with you that night?" asked Victoria.

"Clever girl. The night before the two women disappeared, to be precise. And why do you think he turned up in my lobby? Because his wife had thrown him out of the room! The two of them had had a really bad fight, and he told me about it straight from the horse's mouth. He was furious, but also guilty—I could see that in a second."

"Did he mention what the argument was about?" Tim probed.

"No. I could have got it out of him, of course, if I'd

wanted to. People tell me *everything* after a few glasses. Their whole lives and their dirtiest secrets. I can outdo any shrink! But I wasn't really interested in why the two of them were having a marital crisis. Who cares about that? I was dog-tired on the night in question. I didn't get enough sleep during the day."

"Why is that?" asked Tim.

A smug smile flitted across Alessio's face. "The girls, you know. They keep me on my toes sometimes."

"The *girls*? Plural?" I said to Pearl. "I bet Tracy doesn't know the first thing about that."

"And she certainly wouldn't be happy about it, either," said Pearl.

"But if you ask me," Alessio continued, "it's obvious what the good Mr. Engel and his lady were at loggerheads about. The way he was stalking her sister! The dear wife would've had to be blind to miss it. And stupid if she'd have put up with it."

"Okay, good. So the arguments started that night, not the next day," said Tim. "What else?"

"*What else*? Don't be ungrateful, man! For three hundred bucks that was a really nice dossier. Just like from the cops on TV. Now it's your turn. Do something with it, draw the right conclusions. If I were you, I'd put this Engel character through the wringer instead of chasing a phantom out there in the woods!"

"And how do you think Mr. Engel could be responsible for the disappearance of all the other women?" Victoria objected. "The Killer's Wood didn't get its name just last week."

Alessio sneered. "Yes, that's a pretty scary legend, I'll admit. But who knows how much truth there is in it? People disappearing in a mountainous forest from time to time over many years is unusual for city dwellers at best. Anyone who has grown up here or lived here for a long time has realized that it's simply dangerous out there. *Without* a murderer on the loose. Accidents happen, people fall, they are surprised by bad weather, or they trigger avalanches..."

"Only women?" Tim asked skeptically. "Or why do you think all the victims have been female?"

Alessio groaned in exasperation. "It may sound sexist, but men are more capable off-road. And more sensible when it comes to assessing dangers."

He laughed at his own comment, which somehow reminded me of the neighing of a horse. But then he added: "No, seriously—who's to say that one or two men haven't also had accidents?"

Neither Tim nor Victoria knew what to say to this, which seemed to please Alessio quite a bit.

He casually rested his elbows on the reception counter and continued: "Has it not occurred to you that this legend about the Killer's Wood is incredibly convenient? You could make perfect use of such a superstition if you wanted to get rid of a woman who had become a nuisance. Or even two. Just think about it."

Again, my two-leggeds remained silent.

However, Alessio was now on a roll and couldn't be

stopped. "You've made friends with Mr. Engel, haven't you? Been snooping together? I'll give you some good advice, and it won't even cost you anything extra. Be on your guard and don't just accept this guy as your new best buddy. Maybe he only wants to see what you find out so that he can react in time when things get tight for him. And that could get pretty uncomfortable for you and your sweetheart, my friend!"

24

That night, our two-leggeds sat together with Henrik and Richard in the bar for a long time and discussed the missing persons cases.

We didn't really learn anything new. Both men had zeroed in on Leonard Zauner as the murderer and showed little willingness to even consider other possibilities.

I allowed myself a short siesta, but when I awoke and it was already approaching midnight, I suggested to the tiny one that we take a tour of the hotel.

Our two-leggeds didn't stop us when we left the bar. Both Victoria and Tim looked tired and pretty clueless, but they probably weren't to go to bed yet either.

"Maybe we can track down one or two four-legged witnesses here in the hotel," I said to Pearl as we left the bar and trotted into the lobby.

There was very little going on there at this late hour. Alessio was sitting at reception, so busy with his cell phone that he didn't even notice Pearl and me.

I freely admit it: I didn't like the guy. I would have preferred it if we could have exposed him as the murderer, but so far there wasn't a shred of evidence against him.

Pearl's response to my suggestion to look for animals in the hotel was a little slow and not exactly enthusiastic.

"Four-legged witnesses?" she commented. "There are no pets here. We would have met them by now."

"They don't necessarily have to be pets. Maybe there are rats or mice? You can find them almost everywhere."

"But the hotel doesn't have a cellar," Pearl objected. "Or does it?"

We went in search of a door or staircase that might lead to a cellar vault—but to no avail.

Hmm. Too bad.

After a short break, which Pearl used for personal grooming, we decided to take a tour of the upper floors in the hope that we might be able to eavesdrop on someone through the doors. We also wanted to check on the top floor—where the hotelier's private rooms were located. Was Sissi all right? Did Leonard really have something to hide? And his son Maxim ... he seemed strange to me too, although I couldn't explain why.

At first, it looked as if we would have to leave empty-pawed. All the corridors were deserted in the dim glow of the night lighting. But when we reached the top floor, we came across a two-legged: It was none other than Leonard Zauner.

Pearl and I stopped on the last step of the stairs we had just climbed and ducked down. We didn't want him to notice us.

Not that Pearl really had to duck—she was only as high as the step itself. I, on the other hand, threw myself onto my stomach and then hung quite crookedly over two or three steps. But I accepted that in order to be able to watch Leonard unseen.

Where was he going? To his apartment? Was he just going to bed after a long day? That would have been a let-down.

But to our great luck as top-flight snoops, he was behaving strangely. We wouldn't have been able to tell exactly which door led to his rooms, because we didn't know enough about this floor for that. But he didn't seem to have any intention of going through any door—and that was strange.

Instead, he crept quietly along the corridor, only to stop suddenly in front of one of the paintings that adorned the walls. He fiddled with the top of the artwork with his hand and then pulled a small black something down from there.

Pearl and I were too far away to see exactly what it was, but now was the wrong time to give up our cover and approach the hotelier. We might have startled him and put him off his plan, even if we weren't dangerous witnesses in his eyes.

He pulled something out of his trouser pocket that was even tinier than the black thing and pressed them together. He then stretched his arm up again and placed it back on top of the picture frame.

He seemed satisfied, because now he hurried towards one of the doors at the end of the corridor and disappeared inside.

Pearl and I waited motionless on the stairs for a while longer. Would he return?

The answer was no. The light in the corridor went out by itself.

"Let's go and see what he's put on the picture frame," Pearl meowed softly.

"Go and see? It's pitch black."

"Pah, we cats can see perfectly well when it's dark."

She ran forward—which fortunately caused the light to come on again. This was probably one of the most fascinating bipedal inventions for me, and I even knew what they were called: *sensors*. They were like invisible little eyes that registered movement and then triggered some kind of action. For example, turning on the light.

Pearl and I walked quickly to the picture frame that Leonard Zauner had been tampering with and then raised our heads. But the painting looked completely normal. It showed a summer scene by a waterfall in the mountains. A man and a woman had sat down on a large flat rock for a picnic, and were admiring the natural spectacle before them. The spray from the waterfall looked so real that I expected to get my fur wet at any moment.

There was nothing to indicate that Leonard Zauner had placed anything on top of the frame.

I first had to push myself up with my front paws on the opposite wall to get a better view and then twist my head until I could recognize something.

A tiny black eye seemed to be staring at me from the

top of the picture frame. It looked not unlike a sensor, and thanks to the TV programs Pearl always forced me to watch, I knew it was something similar, something I had often seen in spy movies and crime series. A mini camera!

This allowed a curious two-legged, for example a private detective, to make secret observations, even if he was not in the vicinity.

I dropped back onto all four paws and told Pearl about my find, panting excitedly.

"A camera?" she repeated in astonishment. "Then I know what Leonard has done—he must have fed the thing with a new battery. Otherwise they go on strike and don't record anything!"

As far as I could see, the camera was aimed precisely at the door that I was standing near.

Two questions came to mind: Who lived behind this door? And what did Leonard want from this person? Was the hotel owner really the murderer we were looking for and was he spying on his next victim in this way? The thought made the fur on the back of my neck bristle.

"I think we should direct Tim and Victoria here," I said to Pearl. "They need to see this camera."

"Absolutely. But how are we supposed to make them understand that this thing belongs to Leonard?"

25

I couldn't find an answer to this question, although we did manage to show our two-leggeds the little spy camera that same night.

The opportunity presented itself after we had returned to Tim and Victoria in the bar. They were just ordering *one for the road* from the waiter, which meant that this would be the last drink of the evening, even if they had no intention of going anywhere near a road tonight. I had also learned this from living with humans, although fortunately my two-leggeds were not prone to excessive alcohol consumption. The smell of drunk people is simply nasty—Pearl and I could agree on that for once.

After this last glass of red wine, our two-leggeds said goodbye to Henrik and Richard, who both remained seated and apparently desired to continue their conversation together.

We followed Tim and Victoria into the lobby.

She hooked herself up to him and whispered: "Our two new fellow-snoops are so narrow-minded. How are we ever supposed to find out what really happened? For them, Leonard Zauner is the guilty party and they're not interested in any other leads."

But perhaps the two men were exactly right, I thought. Ever since we had seen the hotelier feeding the mini camera in the hallway with new batteries, I had been inclined to see him as our prime suspect.

Pearl and I went ahead with our plan to lead Tim and Victoria to the painting. I started yapping excitedly and ran towards the stairwell. If we had taken the elevator, it would have been difficult to guide our humans to the right floor.

So we had to work our way up to the top floor on foot. Fortunately, Tim and Victoria were already sufficiently well trained to pay attention to me when I ran ahead of them yelping wildly.

At least that's what I thought, and I was quite proud of it until Pearl suddenly interrupted me: "Um, Athos? Haven't you forgotten something?"

I turned to her. "What is it?" I asked impatiently.

She jumped onto Tim's lap from a standing position. "He's in a wheelchair. He can't take the stairs."

Oh dear. How stupid of me.

"What's wrong, Athos? Where are you going?" Victoria asked me.

"Apparently he wants to show us something," said Tim. That was good, at least he understood what I was getting at.

But Victoria replied: "I realize that, but I'm dog-tired."

"*Dog-tired?*" I repeated indignantly. "But I'm not tired at all! Not when it comes to catching a murderer. And you can be human-tired later, come on, come on!"

I barked a little louder—at the risk of waking a few of the other hotel guests from their sleep.

"Shh!" Victoria hissed. She grabbed my snout with her hand and held it shut. "Don't make so much noise."

I wagged my tail wildly and grumbled a little through my closed muzzle. Of course I could have shaken off her hand, but luckily she understood me—and gave in at last.

"All right, where are you going, Athos?" she asked again. Turning to Tim, she added: "Do you want to wait for me here? Or will you meet me in our room?"

"I'm certainly not leaving you alone in this hotel at night," he said. "See where Athos wants to go, and then I can follow in the elevator. Write me a message!" He pulled his cell phone out of his jacket pocket.

"Okay, I'll do that," said Victoria.

Pearl and I hurried up the stairs. We stopped every few steps to wait for our two-legged, but eventually we reached the top floor and I ran up to the waterfall painting.

I stopped there and this time I stood up against the wall right next to the picture. Then I yelped again, but this time as quietly as possible. I didn't want to end up drawing Leonard Zauner's attention to us. I fervently hoped that he had gone to sleep in the meantime and wouldn't suddenly appear in the hallway.

Pearl dug her tiny claws into Victoria's trouser leg and meowed, which wasn't really helpful, because Victoria gazed down at her instead of looking up at the painting. And so, of course, she didn't understand us at all.

She pulled her cell phone out of her handbag and

must have typed a message to Tim. Less than a minute later, the elevator door opened further down the corridor and he came rolling towards us.

"What is Athos doing here?" he asked Victoria.

"I'd like to know that too. He led me here, to this painting."

I was still standing on my hind legs and leaning against the wall with my front paws.

"Look at the top of the picture frame," I whined.

"Hey, buddy, have you joined the ranks of the art lovers now?" joked Tim. He scratched my head. "Get off the wall, you'll ruin the wallpaper with your claws!"

I barked at the painting, as quietly as I could and at the same time as insistently as possible.

Why did the humans always have to be so slow on the uptake? Admittedly, the camera was tiny and really high up, which made it virtually invisible even to a fairly tall two-legged. Otherwise it would have been discovered by someone long ago and would have failed to serve its purpose as a spying instrument.

Tim would normally have been tall enough to spot the camera, but he was in a wheelchair. I detached myself from the wall, but I wasn't ready to give up yet. I wagged my tail wildly and ran up and down in front of the painting.

Pearl joined me at my side and we ran to and fro together, and then I switched to jumping. And finally, after I must have thrown myself into the air in front of the painting half a dozen times, Victoria had the idea of looking at it up close. She stared at it, ran her hands over the frame, finally stretched out to feel the top edge too—and paused in amazement when her fingers brushed against the camera.

At that moment, the door which was right opposite the painting, in the middle of the mini camera's field of vision, flew open.

Maxim Zauner stepped out. He was wearing a crumpled T-shirt and jogging pants. I had probably woken him up with all my barking. As an impressive almost-wolf, you can't really bark quietly.

"What the...?" he began, rubbing his eyes. "What are you doing?"

Victoria jerked her fingers away from the picture frame. She wanted to say something, maybe talk her way out of it somehow, but in the next moment she probably decided otherwise.

Once again—and this time purposefully—she stretched out her arm, stood on tiptoe and felt at the top of the picture frame for the little thing she had found. She pulled it down and held it out to Maxim.

His face turned into an angry grimace within a breath. "What, a camera?" He snatched the thing from Victoria's fingers.

"I've just found it," she explained to the young man. "Or rather, my animals found it. They led me here."

"Your animals?" Maxim hissed. "Try pulling the other one."

Victoria shrugged her shoulders. Tim intervened.

"We certainly didn't put the thing up there, and unfortunately we can't tell you who's responsible for it, either. But one thing is clear: your room door is right opposite the picture, Mr. Zauner. So apparently you were under surveillance."

The young man let out a curse. He turned the small camera in his fingers.

I couldn't help but get the impression that he wasn't particularly surprised by this find. Or was I just imagining it?

He suddenly seemed to be in a great hurry to get back to his bed. "It's late," he said. "Goodnight."

But Tim wouldn't let him go so easily. "Wait a minute! That's all? *Goodnight*? Someone has been watching you, Mr. Zauner! Spying on you. In a house where guests and employees have disappeared. And you just accept that?"

"Who says I'm accepting it?" Maxim looked older now, somehow. More confident. He stood up to Tim, which was perhaps easy for him in that he could just stare down instead of meeting him at eye level—if Tim had been on his feet instead of in a wheelchair.

"But..." Victoria objected, then Maxim cut her off.

"You're not here with us as private detectives, you're simply on vacation, aren't you? So enjoy your holiday. Don't interfere in matters that are really none of your business."

He closed his fingers into a fist over the mini camera, turned around and disappeared into his apartment.

Victoria wanted to say something more, but the door had already slammed shut.

"How rude," Tim commented—certainly loud enough for Maxim to hear through the door.

Victoria closed her hands around the handles of his wheelchair and pushed him toward the elevator. "Let's get out of here."

She walked a few steps, then looked around for Pearl and me. But we were following her, of course.

When we arrived in our room, the discovery of the camera and Maxim's strange reaction to it left neither Pearl and I, nor our two-leggeds, calm enough to sleep. We speculated about how the incident could be interpreted.

Victoria went first: "Who could have monitored Maxim with that camera?" she asked Tim.

"Who, for how long, and—above all—why, I wonder," Tim replied. "It must be someone from the hotel, that's for sure. Someone who knows where Maxim lives and who can move around the hotel relatively freely. So not just any guest."

"Couldn't Henrik or Richard be behind it?" Victoria objected. "Who knows what investigative methods Henrik has used in his true crime cases. He could also be employing them now in his search for his women."

Tim suddenly smiled. "Now you're saying *his women* too. It's like he has a harem."

The corners of Victoria's mouth twitched. "I have the impression that would be his absolute dream."

"You could be right."

"Here's a suggestion," said Victoria. "We could just ask them if they're behind this—Henrik and Richard, I mean. We're supposed to be partners, so they shouldn't have any secrets from us."

Victoria got up, picked up her cell phone, which was still in her handbag, and started typing a message.

"There, done. I've written to both of them. But they might already be asleep."

The two men seemed to still be awake, even though it must be quite late by now. Henrik's answer came immediately, Richard's only a few minutes later.

Victoria read the two messages to Tim. Both men claimed that they'd had nothing to do with the little spy camera—and both were eager to find out more.

"I'll text them that we're on our way to bed and talk about it at breakfast tomorrow, okay?" said Victoria to Tim.

"Yeah, sure."

But of course, they didn't go to bed, instead continuing to speculate.

Even an hour later, they had not come to an agreement as to who might have installed the camera and for what purpose.

Victoria suddenly changed direction. "I just remembered that Karl, my cross-country instructor, made a strange suggestion," she explained to Tim. "It sounded to me as if Maxim might be interested in Sissi—how shall I put it?—not only as a kind of stepmother."

"I'm sorry, what?" said Tim.

"Karl thought he might have a crush on her." Victoria's expression suddenly darkened. "Karl also said that Maxim hadn't coped well at all with the early death of his mother. That he is a sweet and intelligent young man, but that he has very few friends."

"A loner, would you say?" Tim asked. He brushed a strand of hair from his forehead and looked Victoria questioningly in the eye. "Are you thinking what I'm thinking? Intelligent, early trauma, loner, seemingly very good-natured, has a strange relationship with his father's girlfriend ... you're the psychologist out of the two of us, but that sounds like a serial killer to me."

He raised his hands before Victoria could say anything in reply. "I realize that's a ridiculous cliché. But there's some truth to it, isn't there?"

Victoria nodded. "Of course it's a cliché," she said slowly, "that's been used a thousand times by scriptwriters and thriller authors, and people can't seem to get enough of it. But there are also real serial killers who fit this description—which doesn't mean that Maxim is necessarily a murderer. Let alone a serial killer."

"Sure," said Tim, "but maybe someone suspects him— and that's why they're monitoring him with that spy camera?"

Victoria suddenly turned pale. "Do you think we've been looking at the case the wrong way round? That

Leonard is not our killer, as Henrik and Richard so firmly believe, but it's actually his son?"

"It's possible," said Tim. "What if Maxim detested all the women Leonard grew close to, thereby tarnishing his mother's memory in his eyes? Lucy Zauner may have died of natural causes—in other words she may have suffered an accident—but Maxim never got over it. He was only twelve at the time. And after that..."

"After that, he may have fallen into a deep depression," Victoria said, "not understanding how his father could start relationships or affairs with other women. Until at some point he decided that they had to die..."

"Good heavens, it sounds totally crazy," said Tim. "But it could very well be true."

Victoria's gaze wandered to the window and was lost in the night sky outside. "And now Maxim seems to be quite infatuated with Sissi," she murmured.

"Might that not be a good sign?" Tim asked. "That he's finally able to accept a new woman at his father's side again?"

"I hope so. That would be one possible explanation." Victoria swallowed. "But if we assume that he has psychopathic traits and that he is responsible for the deaths of countless women ... then of course another interpretation would also be conceivable."

"That he's acquired a taste for killing?" Tim said. "And now he's no longer merely angry that his father is entering into new relationships, but that he wants to ... make Leonard's girlfriend his own?"

"Which could end no less fatally for the woman," Victoria said somberly.

26

Our walk with Victoria early the next morning was brief.

Snow was dancing down from the sky in thick flakes, enveloping the mountain landscape in an almost eerie silence. Unlike me, however, our human couldn't bring herself to enjoy it. She was far too preoccupied with her thoughts and shooed us back into the hotel after just a few minutes.

Pearl wasn't happy about this at all.

"Moonshadow still hasn't reappeared," she told me with a most serious face, and if it had been up to her we would have combed half the forest for the lynx on our morning walk today.

But Victoria threw a spanner in the works. She seized Pearl without further ado and took her in her arms.

"Come on, my little ones, back to our room. We'll get Tim and go and have breakfast, okay?"

I have to admit that I was quite hungry, and was already looking forward to the bowl full of delicacies that the nice restaurant staff always had ready for me. And Pearl had even been served her much-beloved salmon in the last few days.

I was all the more stunned when Pearl announced that we would have to skip breakfast today.

I thought I had misheard her. "You want to do *what*?"

I asked incredulously.

"We won't starve if we don't eat something right now," she told me. Pearl, the consummate gourmand.

I blinked and stared at her. Had she been switched overnight, and I'd been given a different kitten?

"Don't look so shocked, Athos! I'm sure our two-leggeds will bring us something if we send them to breakfast alone. And if not, then we'll make a pilgrimage to the kitchen later and I'll get us a snack. The 'kitten about to starve' routine has never failed. If we let our two-leggeds go to breakfast on their own, we'll have enough time to look for Moonshadow in peace, without Victoria calling us back again. The two of them always take forever at breakfast, don't they?"

"That's right," I confirmed. For Tim and Victoria, the first meal of the day wasn't just about eating, but a leisurely affair that they liked to celebrate in peace and quiet. Pearl and I did too, but the tiny one didn't seem to care today.

She was determined to go through with her plan, I could see that in her face. And experienced cat psychologist that I had become, I didn't even try to talk her out of it.

So we returned to our room with Victoria, but both of us—seemingly overcome by a sudden, early morning tiredness—settled down on the bedside rug. We closed our eyes and didn't open them even after Victoria had asked us three times to get up and come to breakfast.

"We'll just leave these two snoozers here and bring

them something later," Tim finally said. He sounded amused, but also a little surprised.

At least we won't starve, I thought.

"All right, darling, if you say so," replied Victoria. "But it's funny. Pearl's not ill, I hope?"

At these words, she got down on her knees and stroked Pearl's head. "I mean, when does our little glutton ever voluntarily skip a meal?"

I had to summon up all my self-control not to roll on the floor from sheer amusement at this remark.

Pearl grumbled, but bravely played the part of the tired kitten. Victoria had no idea how close she'd come to a few painful retaliatory scratches.

"I hope you can get the patio door open, Athos," Pearl groused as soon as the door to the suite had slammed shut behind our two-leggeds.

"Shouldn't be a problem." The glass door was not locked and it had an ordinary handle that you just needed to push down on to open it.

I had to summon up some strength, which fortunately I was able to mobilize without breakfast, and then we were out in the fresh snow.

Pearl trudged ahead and I was permitted to follow her. She scouted and sniffed, called Moonshadow's name and set a considerable pace. Of course, we didn't have forever, even though our two-leggeds liked to have a hearty prolonged breakfast.

It seemed our expedition would not be crowned with success today either. Even after a long search, we were unable to find any trace of Moonshadow.

But the good news was that he found us—some distance from the hotel, in the middle of a dense little fir grove, he suddenly appeared out of nowhere. Again he made a rather dramatic appearance, silently gliding towards us out of the undergrowth like a phantom. Just like a shadow ... he definitely lived up to his name.

Pearl couldn't stop herself. She squealed with delight, ran fearlessly towards the big cat and slapped her pink miniature tongue in his face.

"What luck, you're unharmed!" she exclaimed.

The lynx looked amused. "Of course I'm unharmed. What did you think?"

"I..." Pearl faltered, truly a rare sight. "I ... was just worried about you."

"That's sweet of you," Moonshadow said, "but I'm fine." The way he looked, he was clearly flattered; and suddenly I felt like the proverbial third wheel.

"I've found what you're looking for," were Moonshadow's next words—and that was excellent news after all!

"What, where? How?" I asked, and Pearl rattled off a series of very similar questions.

"I was able to find one of the two women you were talking about ... anyway, I think it's her. She's still very fresh."

"Very fresh?" I repeated, startled. Then she's—"

"Dead, yes," said the lynx. "She fell into a ravine. And

the trees whispered to me that there was violence involved, so she didn't die voluntarily or by accident."

"Murder," meowed Tiny. "That seems obvious! What does the dead woman's hair look like? Is it silver-blond? Or darker?"

"Silver-blond," said the lynx.

"Then it must be Natalia," I concluded.

"And her sister?" Pearl turned to Moonshadow.

"I haven't been able to find any trace of her yet. She's certainly not in the same ravine."

"It's likely the two sisters weren't out in the forest together, remember?" I said to Pearl. "One left earlier, the other a little later."

"One of them could have murdered the other," Pearl mused. "What I'm saying is: maybe Fabienne killed Natalia out of jealousy, because Henrik was so crazy about her. And then she went into hiding so she wouldn't get caught. In that case, it would be only natural that no one could find her body. Not even Moonshadow."

"I'm not infallible either," the lynx interposed. "She could be somewhere else in this forest. I haven't searched the whole area; that would take months. I'm fast, but not that fast."

"You've already done so much for us," I said quickly. "And we're very grateful to you for that."

The lynx gave me a sympathetic look. We still kept our distance from each other, he and I. Respectfully, and in the meantime on quite friendly terms. The big cat, on the other hand, tolerated the tiny one in his immediate vicinity. She sat in front of him and looked up at him with fascinated awe.

Moonshadow had another idea about where Fabienne's body might have gone if she had been murdered too.

"Maybe the murderer buried her," he said. "That's what the two-leggeds like to do with their dead, isn't it? Besides, there are ravines in my territory that even I can't access. Not even the chamois can! And we have caves too. I know them all, but I haven't fully explored some of them."

"Well, a murderous two-legged wouldn't drag a corpse very deep into a cave either," I objected.

"Even in the caves there are ravines ... and bottomless chasms," said Moonshadow.

"Yes, um, of course," I mumbled. This was his territory, not mine. He knew his way around here, whereas I was just a tourist.

"We have to get Tim and Victoria," I said to Pearl, "and lead them to Natalia's body. Then at least they'll know she's really dead and can call the police. And they might find traces on the body that point to the murderer."

"You can forget that," Moonshadow objected.

"Excuse me? I know you don't like humans, and the idea of them invading your territory in droves..."

"That's not the point," the lynx interrupted me. "It's just that you won't be able to guide your two-leggeds into the gorge. You know how insecure they are on their paws because they think they have to balance on their hind legs. They would inevitably break their necks. The terrain is steep and dangerous."

What a bummer. And now what?

I pondered for a moment, then made a spontaneous decision. "Let's do it like this: I'll quickly accompany Pearl back to our hotel room, then I'll come back here and you can show me the way to the body, Moonshadow. Pearl's not much of a climber off-road."

"Nonsense," the tiny one contradicted me immediately. "Of course I'm coming with you! Let's get going, Moonshadow. Tim and Victoria won't be at breakfast forever, and afterwards they'll realize that we've escaped."

The lynx seemed half amused, half impressed by Pearl's drive. He didn't need to be asked twice, however, and set off at quite an ambitious pace.

I had no trouble following him, but I deliberately got in line behind Pearl so that she walked between us—where she was safest.

I was amazed at how brave she was being.

While we soon had to fight our way down a really steep slope, where I slipped more than once and was gripped by dizziness, she kept up the pace without a murmur and complained neither about mud, nor thorns, nor the chasms that kept opening up under our paws.

I could only marvel. What a brave little jungle fighter my tiny one could be. There was no question that she was excited by the discovery of the body, but I suspected that she was also trying to impress the lynx with her intrepid demeanor. And I didn't like that too much.

When we finally stood by the corpse, my stomach tightened. The two-legged lying before us, twisted and with her eyes wide open, was still so young! Her body was in a terrible state, although that shouldn't have surprised me. She had fallen from a great height. No, she had been *pushed*—at least if the lynx had understood his tree friends correctly.

Pearl scurried around and sniffed at her. When she reached the woman's left arm, she meowed excitedly.

"Look, she's holding something in her hand! It's really sparkly!"

I made a leap to reach her side and immediately saw that the tiny one was right: Natalia's fingers were closed into a fist, but a piece of metal with some bright blue gemstones set into it was peeking out.

"A bracelet!" exclaimed Pearl excitedly. She opened her miniature snout and tugged on it.

The thing didn't move an inch.

"Phew, she's really holding on to that."

But it didn't discourage the tiny one. Before I could offer her my help, she had firmly planted her hind paws in the ground and was pulling on the end of the chain with all her strength.

The dead woman's fist finally gave way—revealing an

entire bracelet set with the blue stones along its full length. The metal sparkled as if it had been cast from starlight. It was silvery black, and very finely crafted.

"Look, Athos, here's the clasp," said Pearl. "And it hasn't been opened. The bracelet was torn off! See, right here in this spot." She tapped the chain with her miniature paw. And she was right; one of the chain links had snapped.

A thought began to form in my head. "So if Natalia had been wearing this bracelet herself and it broke off when she fell, she would hardly be holding it in her own fist now."

"Looks to me more like she ripped it off of her killer. Is that what you're saying?" These words came from Moonshadow, who had only come within a lynx's length or two of the woman, but was nonetheless staring at the bracelet, spellbound.

"Yes, exactly," I said. "I think so too. When the murderer pushed her, maybe she got hold of his wrist and ripped the chain off when she fell. So if we can find out who this bracelet belongs to—"

"We'll take it to our two-leggeds," Pearl said resolutely. She grabbed the sparkling piece of jewelry with her snout again and tried to drag it away, but it dangled in front of her in such a way that she tripped over it as soon as she took her first steps.

"Can I take it?" I offered.

She wasn't happy with my suggestion, but at least she was sensible enough not to turn it down. We had no time to lose on the way back, which would be even more difficult than the descent. Tim and Victoria had probably long since returned from breakfast and had found an empty room. The open patio door would at least tell them how we had escaped—which had happened more than once before. Hopefully they weren't too worried about us.

When Moonshadow offered to carry Pearl a little way on the climb out of the gorge to spare her the worst of the hardship, she was having none of it. This suggestion was clearly wounding to her pride and she refused indignantly.

"I'm not a baby anymore," she hissed. "I can walk on my own four paws just fine. Which way do we have to go? Come on, Athos, don't dawdle!"

27

When we finally got back to the hotel, every bone in my body ached. What a grueling hike! And I couldn't even pant properly because otherwise I would have dropped the stupid bracelet.

Of course, Victoria and Tim had long since finished their breakfast. I think it was even approaching lunchtime.

We could already hear them calling for us as we approached the hotel. As I had feared, our absence had been discovered. But at least the voices of our two-leggeds only sounded slightly unnerved and not worried sick.

Moonshadow left us, but not before Pearl made him promise that we would meet again soon. I was relieved that she didn't try to get the lynx to come into the hotel with us.

The tiny one and I trotted the last section of the path, which seemed like a cakewalk after the climb through the gorge, panting side by side and finally spotted Victoria between the trees.

Tim lagged a little behind her in his wheelchair, but from the look of Victoria's shoes and the wheels of his vehicle, they had already covered a considerable distance through the forest.

I was overcome with a guilty conscience, even though

we had made significant progress in our murder case.

"Let me go first," Pearl announced, "Victoria can never be truly angry with me."

I didn't contradict her because I knew she was right. Even if it was highly unfair, of course.

So she meowed loudly as soon as our human was in sight and then ran towards Victoria, while I dropped back a few dog lengths.

"Pearl! Athos! Thank God!" cried Victoria.

She got down on her knees and was about to pick up the tiny one. But she backed away at the last moment. "Oh my goodness, just see how you look!"

"What's wrong with her?" Pearl wanted to know.

"We, um, might have gotten a little dirty." It was a wonder she hadn't noticed. Normally, she would go into grooming mode if she so much as stepped on a speck of dust. But Pearl, the jungle warrior who wanted so much to impress a lynx, was probably cut from a different cloth.

At least until she turned back into Pearl, the cranky sofa cat. Which was exactly what happened now.

"Yuck!" she cried. "You're right, I look terrible."

"Not at all. It's not that bad," I tried to reassure her, but Victoria's expression spoke volumes.

Tim joined us, even if he had to maneuver his wheelchair over a few uneven patches of ground.

He looked just as relieved as Victoria was that we were back, but he still tried to play the role of the stern paterfamilias.

I of course was the target of most of his sermon, because as Pearl had already pointed out, you couldn't be angry with her.

"Athos, are you two crazy? You can't just disappear for hours on end! We really do give you plenty of freedom, but this is clearly going too far!"

I flattened my ears and wagged my tail guiltily. But then I remembered the prize I had brought with me. Tim and Victoria were so upset that they hadn't even discovered the bracelet yet, even though a piece of it was dangling from my muzzle.

I sat down on my hind paws in front of Tim and gently placed the glittering piece of jewelry in his lap. Then I yelped a few times to emphasize the importance of this discovery.

Tim accepted it, puzzled.

"What have you found there, Athos?" He pulled a handkerchief out of his jacket and wiped the bracelet with it. I had probably slobbered all over it during transportation, but recovering the piece really hadn't been a walk in the park!

I was frustrated that I couldn't tell our two-leggeds where and with whom we had found the bracelet. After all, that was the most crucial piece of information.

Could they still do something with it? If Tim and Victoria managed to track down the owner of this piece of jewelry, then Pearl and I had probably found the murderer. But making our humans realize that would be so damn difficult.

"Step by step," Pearl said philosophically. Apparently, she was once again able to read my worries from my face. "We'll catch the guy who owns this bracelet. Our murderer!"

"The *guy*?" I objected. "Guys don't wear bracelets like that. We must be looking for a woman!"

"Yeah, um, that is logical." Pearl looked a little embarrassed that she hadn't already come to this conclusion herself.

However, I have to admit that I hadn't done any further thinking on our murder case either, during the climbing expedition that lay behind us. I'd had to set all my concentration into putting one paw in front of the other without landing in the abyss or getting stuck somewhere in a thicket full of thorns.

"Where did you get this, Athos?" Victoria took the bracelet from Tim and inspected it carefully. "That looks valuable—I think they're real gemstones. And the metal looks like blackened white gold. What do you think, Tim?"

"I don't really have any idea. But yes, it looks expensive."

"Athos must have found it in the forest," said Victoria.

What a realization. You didn't have to be a master detective for that.

How could I make our two-leggeds understand that this glittering bracelet was an important piece of evidence? Possibly the crucial puzzle piece in our murder case?

Now that the thing was no longer dangling from my muzzle and hindering my panting, my conviction grew that Natalia must have ripped it off her murderer's wrist. Her *murderess's*, I should say.

How else could it have gotten into the closed fist of the corpse? Natalia certainly couldn't have found it at the bottom of the ravine, because when she hit the ground, she must have died instantly.

And Pearl and I already doubted that it was her own jewelry—although Henrik could hopefully shed some light on the matter. The way he had openly adored his sister-in-law, he hopefully knew every gem in her possession.

I spun around excitedly and barked again to make it clear to our humans how important this find was.

And to my relief, they seemed to at least halfway understand me.

We returned to our hotel room, where Victoria put Pearl and me straight into the bathtub. Tim watched as we were mercilessly shampooed, and in the meantime got on the phone with Henrik and Richard.

The two of them appeared in our room just as Victoria was rubbing me dry with a large bath towel. I resisted the urge to shake myself because I knew from experience that my human didn't like that at all. I could have dried my fur faster that way, but Victoria would have needed a bath towel herself afterwards.

Tim took over drying Pearl with a washcloth, which wasn't a big problem even with just one uninjured hand. She also kept quiet, although she wasn't a fan of the bathtub any more than I was.

Both Henrik and Richard said that they had never seen the bracelet before, and Richard was sure that it couldn't have belonged to his missing sister, because according to him she didn't care for jewelry at all.

According to Henrik, Natalia and Fabienne loved jewels, but he also maintained quite firmly that the bracelet in question, with its striking blue stones and blackened gold, did not belong to either woman.

Victoria's next step was to question the hotel staff, with us in tow, of course. Tim disappeared with the two men in the meantime, but I didn't realize what they were up to.

We scurried around the hotel, questioned a technician who crossed our path, then the receptionist who was on duty, and finally a few members of staff in the restaurant who were welcoming the first guests for lunch. But none of them had seen the bracelet before.

"Let's ask at the administration office," said Victoria, but when she knocked on the door and entered the office with us, she looked unsure. Because it was Leonard Zauner, of all people, who was there to receive us.

"Can I help you?" he asked stiffly. He probably suspected that we were snooping again—which was true.

But Victoria elegantly pulled herself out of the awkward moment.

"My animals found this bracelet in the forest," she said with a perfectly innocent expression. "It looks valuable, don't you think? Someone must have lost it and would certainly be very happy to get it back. And it could be that this person lives or works here in the hotel, I imagine."

She held out her palm where the bracelet lay. "Have you perhaps seen it before?"

Leonard Zauner's face suddenly looked as if he had been struck by lightning.

"But ... yes I have!" He stared at Victoria, completely baffled.

28

Leonard Zauner blinked, only to fix his gaze in even more astonishment on the bracelet.

"That was a birthday present from me to Sissi," he said. "They are blue spinels set in black gold—a real rarity."

He turned his head and looked at a door that led into the next room.

"Sissi?" he called out loudly.

Immediately afterwards, I heard footsteps and then the door opened. Leonard's girlfriend appeared on the threshold.

"Yes, my darling?" she asked sweetly. She was perfectly dressed again today, as if she had an appointment for an evening at the opera. I didn't even want to imagine how much time she had to spend in front of the mirror every day to look like this.

Leonard took the bracelet from Victoria's palm and held it up.

"Haven't you missed this, sweetheart? You didn't even mention that you'd lost it." His voice was gentle, but it also sounded a little reproachful.

An expression of alarm flitted across Sissi's features—and I stared at the woman as if spellbound.

So *she* had worn this bracelet? *She* was supposed to be our murderer?

"No way," I heard Pearl meow in horror. "She wasn't even on our radar as a possible culprit."

"Shh, let's hear what she says." I was convinced that Sissi must have an explanation at the ready, some kind of proof that this bracelet had had nothing to do with Natalia's murder after all.

She rushed over to us and grabbed the chain.

"Oh my God, where did you find it, darling?" She seemed to be on the verge of tears—but with joy that this piece of jewelry, to which she was apparently very attached, had reappeared.

"Dr. Adler's animals found it in the woods," Leonard said. He seemed angry that the piece had gone missing in the first place, and that Sissi had not mentioned the loss at all. But he was also visibly moved by the vivid emotion written all over her face.

She clutched the bracelet to herself. "I—I lost it while jogging," she confessed contritely. "I looked for it for hours, but I just couldn't find it again."

She bent down and stroked my head. "Such a good dog!" she exclaimed. "We have to give him some kind of reward. What does he like to eat?"—she turned to Victoria—"Steak? Chicken? I'll let him have anything he likes."

"That's very nice of you," said Victoria.

But then Leonard interrupted her: "You went *jogging* with that bracelet on, Sissi? Are you serious?"

The question was of course justified, even if I only realized it now, as a non-jogger.

Sissi's cheeks reddened and she cast her eyes down. "It was very foolish of me, I know! But I love this bracelet so much. It was a gift from you, and I've just never wanted to take it off. I ... it broke my heart when it was lost."

"That hypocrite," Pearl hissed. "It can't just have been lost! Natalia tore it off her, when Sissi pushed her into the depths!"

Somehow I still couldn't quite imagine that, although there was no other explanation. If Sissi had really lost the bracelet whilst jogging, as she wanted us to believe, why had the murdered Natalia been clutching it so tightly in her fingers?

I barked excitedly at Victoria. "This bracelet is a critical piece of evidence! You need to put Sissi through the wringer."

"Hush, Athos, be quiet," was all I got. It was enough to drive you out of your fur!

Leonard was now quite conciliatory towards his girlfriend: "Well, now, the bracelet is back and everything is fine. I'll get it repaired for you, okay? And in future, please take it off when you're doing any sport."

"I'll do that, darling. I promise." Sissi looked completely remorseful and as innocent as a newborn puppy.

It didn't even occur to Victoria that there could be anything wrong with this story. It didn't help that I was yapping my head off.

"Calm down now, Athos," she said to me. "It was very good of you to find that bracelet. Good dog!"

"Give it up," said Pearl. "It's not going to work."

I fell silent. "Then you don't think Sissi is our culprit?"

"What? Of course I do, but Victoria won't get it now. Neither will Leonard. And this Sissi is probably the kind of psychopath who cooks cats, so we don't exactly want to poke her in the nose with the fact that we now know the truth about her. We'll get there."

The cat-cooking thing was a trauma that Pearl had suffered while watching TV, shortly before we'd traveled here to Tyrol, and it seemed to have haunted her ever since. Of course it was her own fault, because she had trained Victoria in such a way that we always had something bloodthirsty on the TV.

In the thriller in question, a morbidly jealous woman—who was merely having a fleeting affair with a man—had uncoremoniously put his wife's cat in the cooking pot, in the couple's own kitchen, where she had sneaked in. It had been an act of revenge because the man had tried to end the affair, while the psychopath saw him as the love of her life.

What a cruel move! Pearl had then refused to watch the movie to the end.

"Couldn't Sissi really have lost the bracelet while jogging?" I mused. "Maybe she's telling the truth after all?"

"It would have had to get caught somewhere, on a branch or something, to tear the bracelet off," Pearl replied. "And she would have noticed that."

"Are you sure?"

"Even if not, think about it: if Natalia had simply

found the piece of jewelry somewhere in the forest, why was she still clutching it so tightly in death? It doesn't make any sense. She would have let go of it at the last when her murderer attacked her. To defend herself, at least reflexively, even if she had no chance."

"Yes, hmm, you're right," I replied. "Clutching the bracelet as she fell into the depths only makes sense if she really did snatch it from her killer. So perhaps Natalia was hoping that she could give the investigators who would find her body the crucial clue to her murderer's identity. After all, she had been an ambitious true crime sleuth in life, so she certainly wanted to ensure in her final seconds that her own death would not remain a mystery forever."

"Exactly. And those investigators are *us*," said Pearl. "Natalia was very lucky—without us, her death might never have been solved."

She corrected herself: "Well, without Moonshadow, to be honest. We could never have done it without his help. He's the hero in this criminal case."

"That's right," I grumbled.

"By the way, Sissi makes perfect sense as a murderer," Pearl added. "Why didn't we figure it out sooner? We didn't even suspect her."

"We assumed that she could be in danger," I objected. "That she might be the killer's next victim."

Leonard Zauner's victim, to be precise. First we suspected him, then his son ... and in between Henrik, and maybe even Richard. But Sissi? Not for a second.

I wanted to bite my own backside. So much for the top detectives that Pearl always made us out to be.

However, she didn't bother with self-criticism, but was already busy pondering further details of the case: "Sissi had probably been in love with Leonard for many years before they became a couple. Didn't she even hint at that to Tracy? And our two-leggeds came up with the idea that Maxim could be jealous of all the women Leonard was with after his wife, i.e. Maxim's mother, died. But Sissi could have been just as jealous, because she wanted Leonard for herself, and she apparently did everything she could to get him. She worked hard on herself, as Karl put it, until she finally became such an irresistible woman that Leonard could no longer ignore her. That's how it must have happened, Athos!"

"And Leonard's wife? Did she really have an accident?" I asked. "Or did Sissi murder her too, so she could get her hands on Leonard?"

"Quite possibly—I would even say quite likely. But one body more or less doesn't really matter. In any case, Sissi has the two sisters on her conscience, Natalia and Fabienne."

"They must have got on her trail," I said. "Natalia mainly, I presume, whose intuitive detective instincts Henrik praised so highly."

"Exactly. And Sissi found out they suspected her," said Pearl. "She had to act quickly before Natalia could expose her. From the looks of it, she lured her into the forest under some pretext, straight into a deadly trap."

I continued the thought: "And when Natalia didn't return to the hotel, Fabienne went looking for her. She didn't talk to Henrik about it, because she was having a bad marital crisis, but just set off alone into the forest. Where she also met her doom. Sissi may have gotten rid of her just to be on the safe side, because she couldn't really know how much Natalia had confided in her—or Fabienne may have come along just as Sissi was pushing Natalia into the abyss."

Pearl meowed excitedly, now visibly in her element as a master detective. "Fabienne might have fled from her for a bit, but Sissi caught up with her. She's damn fit. And then she killed her too, and maybe buried her body or dragged her into one of the caves Moonshadow told us about. That's why we only found Natalia's body in the gorge."

Now everything made sense. Or did it? My head was spinning. So much thinking simply couldn't be healthy.

"Case closed!" cheered Pearl. "We have to go and find Moonshadow right away, and thank him from the heart. Maybe we can dust off a portion of salmon for him in the kitchen, what do you say? Do you think he likes salmon?"

Of course we had the lynx to thank for solving our case, there was no getting away from that, but I still hadn't warmed all that much to the big cat. Maybe because Pearl seemed to be so crazy about him?

I shook myself as if I had just escaped Victoria's bathtub, and quickly pushed the thought of Moonshadow aside.

"Haven't you forgotten something?" I said, to put the brakes on Pearl's enthusiasm.

"What is it?" she asked.

"Well, we first have to make it clear to people that Sissi is guilty," I explained to the tiny one. "So they can put her in prison. And I have no idea how we're going to do that. Do you?"

"No," Pearl had to admit, but she immediately had a solution to this problem at her paw tips.

"Couldn't you just eat her?" she suggested to me in all seriousness. "Why do we always make it so complicated and leave everything to the two-leggeds? We can also ensure justice."

"You're not serious," I grumbled. "Do *I* look like a killer?"

"Why killer? You'd be the judge in this case."

"More like the executioner, you mean."

"Hmm. We could ask Moonshadow to eat her. He doesn't like two-leggeds and wouldn't be so squeamish."

"I'm not squeamish!" I protested. "But vigilante justice is out of the question. A top detective would never do something like that!"

With this I managed to convince her.

"All right then," she grumbled, "we'll just have to take Victoria to the body. And the police as well."

"No way! Victoria would break her neck if we led her into that ravine."

Pearl's whiskers twitched. "Well, I need something to eat first. I just can't think properly on an empty stomach."

29

Sissi insisted that I get a tasty reward for my find, so at least the problem of Pearl's empty stomach was quickly solved. Apart from the fact, of course, that Tiny's stomach could never truly be empty. She was eating and snacking all the time!

Anyway, the murderess accompanied Victoria, Pearl and me to the hotel kitchen and ordered steak for her heroes, as she called us.

After Pearl had taken on a spherical shape and I was also feeling wonderfully full, we decided that we had to shadow Sissi as much as possible. Then hopefully we would have some opportunity to expose her to the two-leggeds as our murderer.

A very vague plan, but we simply couldn't come up with a better one, not even with a full stomach.

When Victoria went cross-country skiing that afternoon, we once again played the tired-out pets and stayed with Tim. Fortunately, he was throwing himself headlong into preparing for his exam and didn't pay any attention to what we were doing, so we managed to steal away again. This time through our suite's main door, not the patio.

We had to wander around the hotel for quite a while

before we met Sissi.

She was sitting with Tracy in the room right next to the hotel kitchen, which was used by the staff as a cafeteria, for meals and breaks. Fortunately, the door—like the kitchen door—was a self-opening model. When you walked towards it, you were detected by sensors and the door slid open sideways. Extremely practical.

Outside in the corridor, we could already hear the voices of the two women, but unfortunately only very indistinctly. Tracy sounded agitated, but was speaking in a whisper.

"We'll go in," Pearl decided, "and snuggle up to Tracy. Giving comfort and all that—it doesn't come across as suspicious. We're just sensitive pets who notice a two-legged's distress and want to help them."

No sooner said than done. We walked through the door, which slid aside in front of us as expected, and then straight towards Tracy.

We were not mistaken, as she had a handkerchief in her hand with which she was dabbing at her eyes, and she seemed to truly be suffering from grief.

I put my head on her knee and Pearl jumped onto her lap. We really were a well-rehearsed team of therapists, and we managed to put a little smile on Tracy's face. Nevertheless, she continued to pour her heart out to Sissi.

The reason for her grief was—once again—Alessio.

"Now he's making eyes at the mommy of this cutie

here!" she complained to Sissi as she stroked Pearl's fur. "He's crazy about her because he thinks she's beautiful *and* clever. How am I supposed to keep up with that? She's got a doctorate, hasn't she? I couldn't be that clever in twenty years!"

"But you're much prettier and younger than that Victoria person, Tracy," Sissi comforted her.

The barmaid wiped away a tear. "Do you really think so?"

"Of course I do. Besides, I've started to find these pets extremely annoying by now."

I received a hostile look. Did Sissi, who had initially appeared to be a true animal lover, suspect or know that Pearl and I were on to her?

I suddenly thought of the cat cooking pot from the TV thriller, except that in my fearful fantasy it suddenly turned into a tub of scalding hot water into which a dog like me could fit quite easily....

Pull yourself together, Athos! I wasn't a scaredy-cat!

I left Pearl to continue comforting Tracy and lay down on the worn carpet that covered the floor. Here in the staff room, there was none of the cozy luxury that surrounded the hotel's guests in their suites.

"You have to fight for Alessio," Sissi advised her friend. "Maybe you should lose a few more kilos? On the hips. And your bottom. And your breasts could be bigger too, my dear."

"Oh no, do you really think so?" Tracy squinted down at her breasts, which really didn't look small in the dirndl dress she was wearing.

"Let's go," I said to Pearl. "There's nothing we can do here."

"Wait a minute. Maybe she'll advise Tracy to elegantly get Victoria out of the way so that she can have Alessio all to herself again. Then Tracy—even if she's not as clever as our human—might realize what Sissi did to get Leonard."

"Sissi won't do something so stupid," I objected.

And I was unfortunately proved right. The conversation went on for quite a while, but our killer didn't say a word. She was unscrupulous, but very intelligent.

How could we put a stop to this dreadful woman?

30

We kept shadowing Sissi, even though she wasn't happy about it at all. More precisely, we accompanied Victoria and Tim to the restaurant for dinner, because Pearl was starving again, but as soon as we had finished our portions, we stole away inconspicuously.

Luck was with us—we bumped into Sissi in the corridor that led to the offices. We followed her at a distance, and quietly so that she wouldn't notice.

She was on her way to the office, I assumed. Maybe to Leonard, who was working late? Or did she have her own work to do?

She had not yet reached the door leading to the offices when it suddenly opened and Leonard stepped out. I caught a glimpse of him before he spotted Sissi; his brow was furrowed and he was holding an envelope in his hand, which he was staring down at angrily.

"Honey?" Sissi ran the last few steps towards him.

He quickly slipped the envelope into the side pocket of his traditional-style jacket. But not quickly enough.

"What's the matter, darling, why do you look so angry? What kind of letter is that?" she demanded.

He forced an awkward smile. "Oh, nothing. Just, uh, an invoice that was issued incorrectly."

Sissi stared at him for a moment—apparently, like me, she thought Leonard was lying—but then embraced him and gave him a kiss on the cheek. "What do you say we go to the indoor pool? And then to the sauna. And then we could..."

He gently untangled himself from her and patted her hand. "Don't hold it against me, love, but I want to go to bed early tonight." He glanced demonstratively at his wristwatch. "It's been a long day and I've got a headache—and I'm in a bad mood, which I really don't want to take out on you."

Of course, I didn't have a timepiece with me. But as Tim and Victoria were still at dinner, it couldn't really be that late.

Sissi was visibly disappointed that Leonard had turned her down, and that didn't escape his notice either.

"We'll go to the baths tomorrow evening, alright?" he suggested. "And then let's have a nice dinner. I'm looking forward to it."

She stood there a little stiffly, but finally said: "It's fine. My poor darling, you really do work too much. Have a good rest." This time she kissed him on the lips, then left him standing there and turned around. Which brought Pearl and me into her view.

The tiny one and I quickly sneaked away and took cover behind the next corner, underneath a staircase. Sissi walked past without noticing us again, while mumbling: "Please God, don't let him have another woman again. I swear, I'll wring his neck this time!"

"Wow!" Pearl exclaimed as soon as she had disappeared. "She probably thinks Leonard has a date with someone else tonight."

"Which is obvious," I said. "He's been a bit of a ladies' man in the past, hasn't he? And he definitely doesn't intend to go to bed early. That was clearly a lie!"

"Absolutely," said Pearl. Her eyes narrowed into slits and she crouched beside me like a sphinx devising a sinister plan.

"Let's keep an eye on Leonard and see who he's meeting with," I suggested. "If he has a secret girlfriend, Sissi is bound to find out ... and then maybe she'll try to kill that woman also. We could catch her in the act."

"Not *maybe*," said Pearl. "But *definitely*. She certainly won't just stand by and watch her Prince Charming cheat on her. This is our chance!"

We ran into the stairwell, hoping that Leonard would take the elevator to return to his private rooms, where he would get ready for his secret rendezvous.

And that's exactly what happened. Just as we reached the top floor, the hotelier disappeared into his apartment.

Pearl and I settled down on the top step of the staircase, where we had taken cover the previous night.

We didn't have to wait for very long. What felt like half an hour later, Leonard's door opened again. He was wearing an outdoor winter jacket and warm boots, so he seemed to be planning to leave the hotel again tonight. Headache and early to bed, my foot....

He took the stairs, which unfortunately meant that he spotted us. There was no way we would have managed to get away quickly enough.

"The way these people let their pets roam around the hotel all the time ... really so inconsiderate," he muttered to himself, but fortunately he didn't bother us any further. He quickly ran down the stairs—and Pearl and I followed him quietly and unobtrusively.

He left the hotel through a back exit that we hadn't even discovered yet, but fortunately the door had a handle on the inside that was easy to push down, so we were able to follow the hotelier at a distance.

Outside, he went down one of the paths that led into the forest.

A night-time rendezvous out here? In this cold? Was he being forced to meet his new girlfriend here for fear that Sissi might find out about this tryst?

We gave him a little head start so that he wouldn't spot us, and only then did we follow his trail.

After a short time, he stopped at a fork in the path and looked around. He hadn't brought a flashlight, but he used the torch function on his cell phone, as the two-leggeds liked to do in the dark.

"Hello?" he called hesitantly. Then he pushed up the sleeve of his jacket and glanced at his wristwatch.

We suddenly heard footsteps approaching from the

right on the path, and then we saw two figures coming towards us, long before the hotelier noticed them. They were dressed all in black. Even their faces were covered with equally dark balaclavas. I had a feeling that these two were not on their way to a romantic rendezvous.

Leonard let out a small scream when the two suddenly stood in front of him. The fact that they weren't showing their faces didn't bode well for him at all.

"Who ... who are you?" he asked uncertainly. "Have you written to me? What do you want?"

"Ah," barked the taller one. "Don't act so innocent. You know exactly what we want!"

"I don't have any money on me," Leonard stammered. "You can't—"

The taller one laughed. "We don't give a damn about your money. We want revenge—served ice-cold, as they say. For all the innocent women you have on your conscience! For Natalia. For Fabienne. And for Beate! And the others you buried here in the forest."

"What? No! You've got the wrong guy!" He pulled the envelope we had already seen out of his jacket pocket, even though we now realized that it was not an invitation to a romantic rendezvous, as we—and Sissi—had wrongly assumed.

"Here," shouted Leonard, waving the envelope in front of the two figures, "I've come because of this letter. Someone wrote to tell me that he knows who killed the women from my hotel. And that I should meet him here today at nine thirty if I want information."

The other masked two-legged laughed.

Pearl and I crept through the undergrowth to get closer to the two black-clad men. I inhaled the air carefully. I knew the scent of the first, larger human. I walked a few steps further, almost silently, and unseen in the darkness. I inhaled the scent of the second two-legged.

Pearl beat me to it again. "Richard and Henrik," she declared, before I could get a word out.

"I know," I replied a little snippily. "I have a nose too!"

Only now, to my horror, did I realize that both men were carrying thick branches in their hands, with which they had no doubt armed themselves here in the forest. Henrik was now swinging his cudgel menacingly in Leonard's direction.

"You're seriously trying to convince us that an innocent man would accept such an invitation?" he barked at the hotelier. "Don't make a fool of yourself! The fact that you've turned up here proves just how dirty you are. You probably thought you could silence an annoying witness—but you were wrong!"

"No. I..."

Leonard didn't get a chance to finish the sentence, because at that moment Henrik's club whizzed down on him.

31

Leonard's scream went straight through my skull and into my spine. In the stillness of the winter night, it even seemed to make the trees around us tremble.

At that moment, I thought I could sense what Moonshadow had told us about: that even those creatures that weren't clad in fur like me, but instead wore bark, could sense human violence and were just as terrified of it as any four-legged.

Leonard stumbled, but raised his arms protectively in front of his face as he fell. He tumbled against one of the giant trees, which halted his fall.

Richard just stood there, instead of supporting Henrik's attack, with his jaw dropped. Apparently he did shy away from physical violence after all, even if he thought Leonard was just as guilty as Henrik did.

But then suddenly there was a third figure wrapped in dark robes—and it too was wearing one of the balaclavas that skiers liked to use to protect themselves from the extreme cold, and which covered the whole face except for the eye area. The figure was a little smaller and slighter than Henrik or Richard, but it lunged at Henrik with determination and pulled him away from Leonard. He fell over backwards, and in seconds the newcomer was upon him, thrusting a knife blade under his chin. "Don't even flinch, you bastard, or you'll regret it!"

I held my breath—no, I howled. Somehow both at the same time, although that should actually be impossible.

"Oh dear salmon," I heard Pearl say next to me, who seemed to be as frozen to the forest floor as I was.

And then, as if the chaos wasn't already extreme, a fourth human suddenly came running up—wearing normal clothes and with just an ordinary cap on his head. It was Maxim Zauner. When he reached the others, however, he didn't really know what he meant to do, it seemed to me.

I barked, purely out of reflex—and that at least got Richard to shout "Stop! Everyone step back!"

"That's Sissi who jumped on Henrik to defend Leonard," I heard Pearl's voice saying.

In the next moment, she pulled the blade away from Henrik's throat and pushed him away. Then she jumped up, ripped the balaclava from her head and stared at the newcomer: "Maxim? But..."

Leonard also got to his feet again, and only Henrik lay there as if he had been the actual victim of this scuffle. But at least he and immediately afterwards Richard also pulled their caps off their heads.

"Shut up, you stupid dog!" Sissi yelled at me—and only then did I realize that I was still barking like crazy.

I fell silent, more out of shock than out of obedience to this disgusting woman. She was the monster in this Killer's Wood, not Leonard! How could I make the two-leggeds understand that?

The sobering answer was: not at all.

Henrik finally got back to his feet, and his desire to fight was not yet completely gone. He addressed angry words to Sissi: "Your partner is a murderer of women, you must realize that! You should put the blade to his neck, not mine!"

Sissi looked ready to pounce on Henrik again, like a lioness about to defend her mate with tooth and claw.

But Maxim suddenly stood next to her and grabbed her by the arm. "He's right, Sissi! Father is a murderer. We cannot look the other way any longer."

"Have you lost your *mind*?" Leonard roared.

"You need to confess at last, Father!" Tears were suddenly streaming down Maxim's cheeks.

Which finally freaked out the hotelier.

"You want me to confess?" he snapped at his son. "After everything *you've* done, now you want to pin it on *me*? When I've spent all these years trying to protect you, to heal you from your sick—"

"Cure me? What are you talking about?" Maxim cut him off.

"Oh please, enough of these stupid games! You were in the forest the afternoon that Fabienne and Natalia disappeared. I saw you coming back. You're always hanging around out here—"

"But only because of you! So that you don't kill another woman. Like Mother, or all the others you've had an affair with! When you get tired of them..."

Leonard's mouth fell open. He probably wanted to

throw another vile accusation at Maxim, but something gave him pause.

There was a stillness, during which he stared at his son, stunned. And the young man stared back, equally shocked and dumbfounded.

Finally, Leonard broke the silence—in a calmer, albeit very emotional tone. "You seriously thought I had ... that I could kill someone?"

"Didn't you...?" Maxim's words were no more than a whisper. He wiped the tears from his face with a shaky motion of his hand, and looked as if his knees would give way at any moment.

The other two-leggeds stood by in amazement, unable to utter a single word. Only Sissi seemed to have herself under control, but she didn't interfere either.

"My boy," Leonard stammered. "I really thought that you—"

His voice failed him. "You've been acting so strange since your mother died," he croaked. "And every time I fell in love with a new woman, you became so hostile..."

"I missed Mom! That's normal. I still miss her and maybe it will never stop—what am I supposed to do about it?"

"You're already twenty and you still don't have a girlfriend. Not even any male friends," Leonard said hesitantly. "That's ... strange."

"Then I'm just weird!" exclaimed Maxim. "A loner. But that doesn't make me a killer."

"I loved your mother just as much as you did," said

Leonard. "I just tried to get over her death in a different way."

"By becoming a Casanova? By taking one woman after another to bed?"

"I just never found the right woman," Leonard defended himself.

"Your *women* ... are all dead now, Father," Maxim gasped. "That can't be a coincidence. And last night I found out that you had installed a camera outside my room. It was you, admit it! So that you always know where I am and I can't get in your way? Did you want to kill Sissi too?"

"What? No!" Leonard looked completely confused by now. "Yes, it was me with the camera. I wanted to know what you were doing when you leave your room and go into the woods. Where you ... hell, I really thought you'd done something to all those women!"

Suddenly, Leonard also had tears streaming down his cheeks. "Have I suspected you wrongly, my boy?"

Maxim swallowed. "And I you?"

The two of them looked at each other as if each was seeing the other for the first time.

There was a reticence lurking in their eyes, which looked big and full of fear in the light of the cell phone flashlights. But they were also full of longing that the other might be innocent after all. Both men seemed hopeful now to me that they could win back a father or a son whom they hadn't trusted for years. They had believed the very worst, namely that the other was a serial killer.

It would be some time before the two of them could fall into each other's arms and become a family again, but with their fear and caution, their anxieties, but also their desire to trust each other, they finally convinced Henrik of their innocence. Richard looked a little more skeptical at first, but in the end he lowered his arms with a groan. He threw away the cudgel he had armed himself with.

"They didn't do it, neither the father nor the son," he whispered to Henrik. "We were on the wrong track."

"Looks like it," Henrik grumbled. "But who then?"

"I wish I knew, man." Richard pressed his lips together in frustration until they became a thin white line.

"We know!" Pearl meowed excitedly, but none of the two-leggeds paid any attention to her. "It was Sissi! She followed Leonard into the forest tonight because she thought he was going to meet up with a new, secret lover. And she took a knife with her. Why doesn't he understand that, Athos? Is he really that stupid?"

"He just loves her," I said. "And is completely blind to her faults."

"She probably would have killed *him* this time, Athos. Do you remember what she said back at the hotel when she left Leonard?"

"'I'll wring his neck this time'." The whispered threat, when she thought she was unobserved, was still fresh in my mind.

"Yes. But the important thing is how she emphasized the words! She didn't say: 'I'll wring his neck *this time*,' as if she had been hesitating to do that earlier. She said: 'I'll wring *his* neck this time.' So not his supposed new lover's! Or at least not only hers."

Pearl's nose twitched with excitement. "She's our murderer, Athos, that just confirms it! She wouldn't shy away from killing Leonard, after all she's already done for him in her eyes—years of working to make herself beautiful enough for him—so that he would finally notice her, even though she had been loyal to him for so long."

"All those women had to die because they got in her way," I moaned.

Pearl ran over to Sissi and clawed at her trouser leg, snarling.

Sissi didn't even notice at first. And when she did spot Pearl, she just grinned.

"Oh, you little rascal! It's irresponsible of your master and mistress not to take better care of you. A kitten so small doesn't belong in a forest at night."

She bent down and pulled Tiny away from her trouser leg, although Pearl clung to her with all her might. My brave little master detective simply didn't have the strength to resist a two-legged.

I was immediately at her side. "I'm taking good care of Pearl," I growled at Sissi. "And you're the only danger in this forest!"

The two-leggeds didn't understand me at all. Maxim

and Leonard even teamed up together to shoo me away.

"What a big aggressive mutt!" commented Henrik.

And Sissi? I saw her smiling haughtily to herself. When our eyes met, she seemed to mock me. *You ridiculous creatures will never convict me! I'm much smarter than you.*

Pearl and I left with our heads hanging low. This round had gone to the murderess—but we weren't ready to admit defeat just yet.

32

"What if we *pin* the murders on Sissi?" Pearl suggested when we were lying sleepless that night on the bedside rug.

After we'd returned to them, Tim and Victoria had had a long chat with Richard and Henrik, who of course had told them all about the incident in the forest.

Leonard had refrained from pressing assault charges against Henrik, and in the end the two men even shook hands and made peace.

We couldn't count on our humans to solve this murder case; they were now more in the dark than ever. So it was up to Pearl and me to hunt Sissi down.

"You want to do *what*?" I exclaimed upon Pearl's suggestion.

Outside the window, new snow was quietly and majestically falling again, and the steady breathing sounds coming from our two-leggeds should have helped to calm me down. Normally they did, but not tonight. I couldn't and wouldn't relax as long as a bloodthirsty murderess was threatening to get away with all her crimes.

"Well, pinning something on somebody ... that's what murderers often do," the tiny one explained to me. "They lay false trails to innocent people, to divert attention from themselves and blame their crimes on someone else. So what if we fox Sissi in this way, incriminating her for her own murders? We plant some piece of evidence in her room, something that belonged to one of the victims, and then we let our two-leggeds find it? Or the police, for all I care. Someone would just have to give them an anonymous tip."

"And who is this someone supposed to be?" I grumbled. "Are you going to meow into the phone?"

"Are you in a bad mood, Athos?"

"What? Yes, of course, aren't you?"

"We'll manage," she said—but wasn't she looking over at that patio door again?

It was only a brief movement of her head, after which she turned her eyes back towards me. They looked bright even in the dark, but the thought immediately popped into my head that she must be thinking of Moonshadow again. Would he have been a better partner than me in this murder case? Would she have liked to run out into the night, into the cold and the snow, to consult with him?

The lynx might not have hesitated, and would possibly have killed Sissi without further ado. *Case successfully closed.*

I pulled myself up from my prone position and sat on my hind paws. I wasn't a loser who'd just give up!

And maybe Pearl's suggestion to plant evidence on Sissi wasn't as crazy as it sounded.

"Let's think about this," I said to her. "What could we plant on Sissi that would arouse the investigators' suspicions?"

"A weapon? Something that belonged to one of the victims?" the tiny one replied promptly.

I panted a little because it was once again terribly hot in the room, and tried to concentrate.

"Well, as far as the weapon is concerned," I said, "that could be difficult. Officially there are no bodies. And Natalia, the only one we've found, was simply pushed into the abyss. So what are we supposed to slip to Sissi?"

"Hmm. Well," Pearl said, "if they found a gun on her or, say, poison, that would at least be suspicious. Then the two-leggeds would probably think she was planning a murder, and then they'd finally take a closer look at her as far as the murders in the past are concerned."

Tiny's train of thought was coherent, and actually quite clever. The idea of framing a murderess in this way had something to it, I thought. There was just one tiny problem.

"How on earth are you or I supposed to get poison or a gun, Pearl? Or any weapon at all?"

Unfortunately, my feline master sleuth didn't know the answer either.

She dropped her head onto my paw. "I'm going to sleep now. The two-leggeds are simply too stupid to understand us. Let them murder each other. I don't care!"

Now we were both frustrated. It wasn't long before Pearl started snoring.

However, I still couldn't get any sleep. Nevertheless, I fell into a strange state that resembled a dream—and suddenly that ghastly movie I've already told you about was playing in front of my inner eye: the TV thriller in which a psychopath had put her rival's cat in the cooking pot.

I bolted upright with a yelp.

"Athos, what's wrong?" Victoria mumbled in her sleep. She rolled onto her other side on top of the bed, but then continued to breathe evenly.

I'd awoken Pearl, however, because I had pulled her pillow—my paw, that is—away when I jerked up.

She hissed—she could do that even when she was only half awake—and the next moment she opened her eyes and looked at me reproachfully.

"What's going on?" she mumbled.

"I have an idea, Tiny!"

"What ... you do?"

"Hey, don't be cheeky!" I gave her a shove with my muzzle.

She rolled theatrically to the side. "Ow, ruffian!"

"Drama queen!" I countered. "And now listen to me. We're not going to plant something on Sissi, we're going to plant it on Leonard!"

"But he's innocent," muttered Pearl, still quite sleepy.

More radical measures were called for to get her fully awake. I needed her full attention, even if it meant risking a scratched nose.

Bravely, and as inconspicuously as possible, I opened my mouth—and slapped my tongue right in her face. Then I jumped to the side to get out of the line of fire.

And I was quick enough! Her paw swipe came to nothing. Ha!

"Listen to me, Pearl!" I called out quickly. "You remember the movie with the cooked cat..."

"How dare you..."

"No! It's not about the cat. Forget the cat. I mean, of course: poor cat! And what an unspeakable outrage to cook it—but my point is, do you remember what made the psychopath so insanely jealous that she killed her rival's cat? And she probably attacked the woman herself later, too, when we were no longer watching. I'm sure of it."

After all, thanks to Pearl, I had already seen an almost endless number of such films. By now I had a certain amount of practice in predicting plot elements.

Pearl's whiskers twitched. Her nose glistened damply in the moonlight that fell on the floor. My wake-up call had left its mark.

"Hmmm," she said, "so the psychopath found a pair of the wife's panties in the husband's, that is her lover's, car. I have no idea why a guy would start an affair with a psychopath only to have sex with his own wife again—and in the car to boot. That must be terribly uncomfortable. As I always say: they're crazy, these two-leggeds."

"Yes, yes, I know. But that's just what I'm getting at, Pearl!"

"That the humans are crazy? And you subject me to a full face bath for that?"

"The *panties*, Pearl!" I cried. Sometimes she could be really slow on the uptake. "We have to slip Leonard a pair of panties and make sure Sissi finds them. Then she'll be convinced that he's cheating on her. She'll be raging with jealousy and then finally try to kill him. Which she already meant to do when he got the letter from Henrik and Richard, but she thought it was from a new girlfriend."

Pearl's ears twitched. "Not a bad idea. But sacrificing Leonard to get to her? Isn't that kind of ... inhumane? You might as well eat Sissi, I think. Why go to all this trouble?"

"I don't want him to die, Pearl," I moaned. "He's a man, so he's not completely defenseless. And I—I mean *we'll* protect him, of course!

"Yes, we will," said Tiny.

She scratched her chin with her hind paw and seemed to ponder my idea in more detail. "Sissi will expose herself as a crazed murderer if she tries to kill Leonard," she muttered.

"Exactly," I said. "And that's how we'll get her!"

"Then all we need now is a pair of panties," said Pearl.

"It's much easier than finding a gun," I explained to her. "We'll just steal a pair from Victoria—she won't even notice. And then we'll sneak into the hotel office, unseen. We'll hide the panties in Leonard's desk, and then we'll make sure Sissi finds them there."

The plan wasn't child's play by any means, but it was somehow feasible. At least in my imagination.

"This one requires finesse, advanced sneaking and a good amount of silent pawing," Pearl said. "I'll take care of that."

Who else?

She was already scurrying off into the hallway and to the cupboard where our two-leggeds had stored their clothes.

I was allowed to follow her like a valet who had to run a few steps behind his mistress. But I wasn't complaining; we had finally found a way to possibly catch Sissi after all.

"Victoria's panties are in the second drawer on the left, aren't they?" she mused.

"I think so."

"Open the drawer!" she ordered.

"Yes, Madam General! Very well! Always at your service."

My sarcasm—as almost always happened—went right over her little fluffy head.

She actually said *good dog* to me when I managed to pull open the drawer, as if she were my two-legged. Where would this all end up, I asked myself, and not for the first time.

I stuck my snout into Victoria's lingerie collection and hesitated briefly, not knowing which panties would be best for our battle plan.

She had recently bought a whole range of lingerie in purple lace, which I had often seen her wearing. Now in the dark the lingerie looked almost black, but the color wasn't important. Lace was good. I knew that men loved it when women wore lingerie with lots of lace. For some strange reason.

"Take the one with the least fabric," Pearl ordered.

"And you think I can see that here in almost complete darkness?" I mumbled, my snout buried deep in the drawer.

"The smaller the panties, the more men like them," Pearl lectured. "Haven't you noticed that yet?"

She was right. That was another crazy habit of the two-leggeds. On the one hand, they loved to dress up in God knows what—probably out of a deep sense of inferiority because they hardly had any fur. The women in particular spent huge sums on more and more clothes. But on the other hand, their underwear couldn't be tiny enough, when it came to impressing a man.

How much easier it was to be a dog, with the same magnificent coat for all situations! Okay, sometimes I would have liked to slip out of it in the hottest days of summer, but otherwise we were really much better off than the two-leggeds.

I grabbed one of the panties, none of which were big anyway, and dropped the booty on the floor by Pearl. Then I pushed the drawer shut again. Hopefully Victoria wouldn't notice the next morning that I had rummaged through her lingerie, but as a detective you have to take risks like that.

I grabbed the panties off the carpet again, carried them into the bedroom and hid them under the couch.

"Now we just have to smuggle them into Leonard's office without being seen," said Pearl.

"We'll manage," I replied, although I was feeling pretty queasy about such a challenge.

33

Pearl and I were hoping that Leonard would perhaps go to his office early the next morning and that we would be able to smuggle in the telltale piece of lingerie then.

So we tried our luck when Tim and Victoria decided to go to breakfast.

Of course we couldn't walk out of the room right next to our two-leggeds holding the treacherous thing in my teeth, so Pearl and I came up with a breakneck move that I must admit I was a little proud of. If it worked, that is.

First I distracted Tim and Victoria at the exact moment when Victoria had already opened our suite door and Tim wanted to roll out into the corridor with her.

I yelped loudly and then threw myself onto Tim with my front paws and started to give him kisses.

"Oh gross, Athos!" he shouted with a laugh—just as I had expected. As one of his arms was still in plaster, he couldn't really defend himself against my wave of hairy affection. Victoria came to his aid, also laughing, and tried to pull me off his lap.

But a strong almost-wolf can certainly resist such an attempt for a while. Time enough for Pearl, who at that moment, without the two-leggeds even noticing, galloped past us—with the delicate piece of cloth in her muzzle. She ran ahead to the stairs, I gave her a bit of a head start and when I could no longer see her, I gave up besieging Tim and galloped after Pearl.

"What's wrong with Athos this morning?" I heard Victoria's voice behind me.

Pearl and I ran down the stairs. I took over carrying the panties now because, after all, her snout was tiny and I didn't want her to choke on the piece of underwear or trip over it if she let it hang out too far between her feet.

At a wild gallop, we reached the corridor on the ground floor, where the offices used by both Leonard Zauner and his most important employees were located. Our destination was the room where his desk was situated.

I handed the panties back to Pearl outside in the hallway and let her take cover behind a potted plant.

Then I started scratching at the office door, desperately hoping that someone was already there. Preferably Leonard himself, because I didn't know whether his room door inside the office might not have been locked, at least before he went in there for the first time in the morning.

I was lucky! The hotelier personally opened the door for me.

I stormed straight past him to get his attention and Pearl took the chance to slip through the door before Leonard let it close.

He only had eyes for me, the annoying mutt who was causing him trouble again. He ran a few steps after me, swearing.

I didn't want to scare him, so I didn't jump on him to keep him busy, but threw myself on my back, bared my belly and stretched out all four paws, panting happily.

Play with me! This message could be understood by almost every two-legged, whether they were animal lovers or not.

Leonard wasn't one, so he didn't squat down to scratch my belly, but I didn't care. I had his attention and that was all that mattered. Out of the corner of my eye, I saw a white ball of fur with a piece of purple fabric hanging out of its mouth dart towards the hotel manager's desk. Pearl and I had agreed that she would hide the *corpus delicti*, the panties, under this piece of furniture.

In record time, she had put the plan into action and was now trudging towards me and Leonard with an innocent face.

"Where have you come from now?" groaned the hotelier when he saw Pearl. He had no idea for a second that she had sneaked under his desk like a top-class spy.

I rolled around and jumped up. And as if we were suddenly the most obedient pets ever, Pearl and I trotted straight to the door.

"Ha!" Leonard exclaimed. "Good idea, get out of here and let me work in peace!"

He opened the door for us and we strolled off. Phase one of our daring plan had been successfully completed.

We tackled phase two in the afternoon, when Victoria had another cross-country skiing lesson with Karl. We again behaved like tired pets who would rather stay in the hotel than romp around outside, and then escaped at the first opportunity when Tim left us unattended.

We repeated the crazy game at the office door that we had already played in the morning. This time there were two of us. I scratched at the door; now it was Sissi who opened it, and Pearl and I chased straight to Leonard's desk.

He literally exploded with rage. "Not these two again! What are these people thinking, leaving their pets unattended all the time? Do they have no manners at all? Maybe we should think about allowing any more animals in this hotel," he shouted to Sissi, who had just come running in after us.

I almost felt sorry for Leonard by now, but at least we were trying to free him from the murderess he was in love with. The bottom line was that he was going to be grateful to us, I told myself.

Pearl and I started playing tag around his desk until she—being the shy kitten that she is—took refuge underneath.

When she reappeared, she had the panties between her teeth and, apparently quite unintentionally, ran straight in front of Sissi's legs. We were both really Oscar-worthy, I thought.

Sissi reacted exactly as Pearl and I had imagined. She immediately recognized what Pearl had apparently found under Leonard's desk—and gave him hell.

I'd rather leave out the unpleasant details of the argument that ensued between Sissi and Leonard at this point.

Sissi stormed out of the office shortly afterwards—followed by the two of us, of course—and when she thought she was out of earshot of witnesses, she cursed: "I *will* wring that bastard's neck!"

That was music to our ears, and the starting signal for phase three. Now we just had to make sure that Leonard, our poor decoy, didn't die while we hoped to finally expose Sissi as a murderer.

We stayed close to her, unseen, as far as we could. At first she retreated to her room, where we could hear her crying her eyes out.

I almost felt sorry for her, but when she had calmed down a bit, she left the room and unexpectedly went about her duties in the hotel. She checked the work of the chambermaids, spoke to one or two of them and seemed to have regained her emotional control.

But then, when the tiny one and I escaped again towards the end of dinner, while Tim and Victoria were still sitting down to dessert, we had to watch our wonderful plan, prepared with such careful paws, go down the drain in the worst possible way.

At first we didn't think anything of it when Sissi spontaneously gave the chambermaid, who was assigned to the evening service in the guest rooms today, the night off.

"You always do such a wonderful job, Ines," she said to the woman. "You can take the evening off tonight and I'll take care of the rooms."

The evening service—which Pearl and I had already seen for ourselves—involved the bed being made up again and turned down so that the guests only had to slip under the covers later on. A small chocolate was also placed on each pillow. This didn't take much time, so a single employee was able to perform this service in all the suites.

Sissi, however, seemed to take a relatively long time when she went into the first guest room.

We kept our distance from her, hid in the hallway behind decorative chests of drawers and potted plants, which fortunately were standing around there, and were thus able to keep an eye on our murderess without being seen ourselves.

She went into one room after another. Sometimes she finished very quickly, sometimes she took longer. But she had to do the same thing in every room, didn't she?

At some point, I couldn't stand the tension any longer. I had to know what she was doing in the rooms and why she had so willingly taken the evening service from Ines. Somehow, neither Pearl nor I believed that she had done it out of pure kindness.

When she finally arrived at our own room, number four, Pearl and I decided to follow her into the room. After all, we lived here, so it wouldn't be particularly noticeable if we suddenly appeared.

As soon as she had opened the door with her key card, I left our hiding place and stormed over the threshold behind her. Pearl whizzed past me and then we were in the anteroom together with Sissi as the door closed behind us.

She hardly noticed us. So far so good. As I said, this was our two-leggeds' room and we had every right to be here.

But what she did next made my blood run cold. Instead of going into the bedroom to prepare the bed for the night and put chocolate on the pillows, she went straight to the wardrobe in the hallway.

She pulled out the drawers in quick succession and my heart almost dropped into my hind paws. It dawned on me what she was looking for here, what she had been looking for in all the previous rooms.

The answer was—panties. She was obviously trying to find out whose lace underwear Pearl had "found" under Leonard's desk.

She pulled open the drawer that I had rummaged through just last night. The drawer that contained Victoria's lingerie. And then a diabolical grin suddenly flitted across her face, causing me to let out a startled yelp.

She lifted up one of the purple lace panties as if it were the most disgusting thing she had ever held in her hands.

"I've caught you, you bitch!" she whispered. "You'll pay for that!"

She let the panties fall back into the drawer and slammed it shut. "I guess making eyes at Alessio wasn't enough for you, huh? But you'll be so sorry that you made a pass at my Leonard. I swear to you!"

34

Pearl and I ran after Sissi when she left our room. Enraged as she was, she hadn't made the bed or placed any chocolates.

Now, out in the corridor, her eyes were glittering with hatred, but she still managed to get herself back under control.

She fiddled with her traditional costume for a moment, smoothed out her apron and then hurried on to the next room.

This woman would not neglect her duty, come what may. And she wouldn't murder her Leonard either, as Pearl and I had assumed, I now realized to my utter horror. She probably loved him far too much for that, no matter how often he might turn to someone else.

But what fate awaited this other woman—the *supposed* other woman whom Pearl and I had invented—there could not be the slightest doubt. Sissi would not rest until she lay dead at the bottom of some ravine. In the Killer's Wood, which owed its name to Sissi's raging jealousy.

And this new victim of the ice-cold murderess was to be our Victoria.

Pearl and I left Sissi to her work and ran back to the

restaurant.

"We have to watch Victoria around the clock from now on," I said to Pearl. "Sissi mustn't harm a hair on her head!"

"Tough luck. Now our own human is our bait."

"Tough luck? It was irresponsible of us to take Victoria's panties! We should have foreseen that it could go wrong. It *had to* go wrong with this lunatic, who is also the housekeeper here at the hotel. Who can go snooping in every room without anyone noticing."

"We'll look after Victoria," said Pearl. I didn't know where she got her composure from.

Sissi didn't hesitate for long. The very next morning, she had apparently devised a diabolical plan to kill our human.

She appeared in the forest when Victoria took us for our morning walk. She was wearing a jogging outfit and came running towards us like the devil was after her. We hadn't gone too far from the hotel yet.

"Oh, it's you, Dr. Adler! Heaven sent you," she gasped as she stopped less than two steps away from Victoria.

I growled, but Pearl kept her cool.

"This is our chance," she told me. "Probably our only one. We can't afford to make a mistake."

"Chance? No, Pearl! Victoria and this lunatic here all alone in the forest? I'm not going along with that. We have to get her out of here, to safety!"

"And where would that be?" replied the tiny one. "Sissi will look for her—and find her, you realize that, right? She won't just give up once her jealousy has been kindled. Think of the psychopath in the movie! We have to get her here and now, or do you want her to put me in a cooking pot too before she goes for Victoria's throat?"

Once again, she was right, from a sober point of view. But I just kept growling, I couldn't help it.

"Quiet, Athos," said Victoria. "What's wrong?"

I hoped that she would understand the danger she was in, that she would interpret my growl correctly after all the murderers we had already had to deal with.

She at least gave me a questioning look, but then Sissi intervened again—and unfortunately in a very clever way.

"Oh, he can probably sense that I'm completely out of my mind!" she exclaimed, managing to look like an innocent little mouse who had just encountered a monster and was beside herself with fear.

"I found something on my morning round," she explained to Victoria in a quivering voice. "No, I deviated from my usual path. I couldn't say why. Female intuition, perhaps? Anyway..."

She put her hands on her hips, leaned forward slightly and gasped. "I'm sorry. It was such a horrible sight!"

"What have you found?" Victoria looked alarmed, but I could see that her curiosity was also aroused. And the hope of perhaps making a decisive breakthrough in our seemingly hopeless murder case after all.

"A ... dead body," Sissi stammered. "Half buried in the ground. An animal must have dug it up. I think it's one of the missing women. Fabienne Engel. But I—you have to see this. It's..."

"Have you got your phone with you?" asked Victoria. "I left mine in the room; I just wanted to go out with Athos and Pearl. We have to call the police immediately!"

Sissi shook her head. "I never take my cell phone with me when I go jogging. And before we call the police, you should..."

She broke off and groaned again. "It's so strange. You'd think the culprit—oh, come and see for yourself. It's not far and I don't think we're in any danger. You've got your dog with you."

What a snake. She was taking advantage of my presence to lull Victoria into a false sense of security. And that wasn't all!

She suddenly put her right hand in her jacket pocket. I growled again, assuming she was about to pull a weapon out of it. The jacket she was wearing had large pockets, and they were clearly not empty. They bulged out a little on either side of her body.

What she fished out, however, was aluminum foil with little balls inside. "Here, I always take this for the squirrels, I love feeding them. But maybe your pets will like them too?"

She didn't wait for Victoria to give her consent, but

bent down to us and held one of the balls out to me first.

It smelled delicious and like meat. It certainly wasn't traditional squirrel food. Sissi must have prepared it especially for Pearl and me to knock us out, I was sure of it! She must have put some kind of poison in the mixture.

"Don't eat under any circumstances!" I hissed to Pearl and growled again. I simply couldn't control myself in the presence of this devious killer.

"I'm not stupid," came Tiny's reply. She also refused to accept the supposed treat.

"Athos, what's wrong?" Victoria gave me an uncertain look.

She said to Sissi: "I'm sorry. He's not usually so rude." She didn't say a word about Pearl's behavior. She was probably not surprised that the tiny one was picky when it came to food.

Rude? went through my head. I had to summon up all my self-control not to bite Sissi's hand when she tried to poison me with such hypocritical friendliness.

Sissi looked uncertain for a moment, but then she put the balls back in her pocket and grinned wryly. "It's probably not the right thing for your two. You're not squirrels. But come on, there's no time to lose."

She led us deeper into the forest and Victoria followed her without hesitation. Nevertheless, I noticed that she no longer smelled merely excited and curious, but clearly anxious. Was she beginning to suspect that Sissi was playing a false game with her?

She looked down at me several times as she continued to follow Sissi. If I hadn't been with her, she might have tried to return to the hotel under some pretext by now.

I stayed very close to her side. I had to react at the first wrong move the murderess made. Every second, any moment of hesitation could now decide Victoria's life. Or her death. I wondered what weapons Sissi was carrying.

"Is it still far?" Victoria asked a few minutes later. "Didn't you say it was very close?"

"We're almost there. Just a little way up here."

"You're in very good shape," Victoria gasped, still following the assassin. "You're not even out of breath." By now she clearly sounded nervous.

"I jog every day," replied Sissi. "You build up a certain level of fitness."

Up. Out of breath. The words only seemed to find their way into my head now. We had been walking steeply uphill for a while. And that could mean that an abyss was lurking at the end of this ascent. *That* was Sissi's weapon, which she had used more than once. Not least with poor Natalia, who was now lying at the bottom of a ravine.

My growl became a startled yelp, then a whimper. I licked Victoria's hand. "We mustn't go any further—it's far too dangerous!"

Pushing someone into the abyss could happen so quickly; I was completely powerless against it.

I stopped and didn't want to let Victoria move on.

But to my horror, I realized that Sissi had also stopped. And what was even worse: The forest was already clearing behind her and the sky could be seen. My worst fears seemed to be confirmed. Nothingness lurked just a few dog lengths away from us—certain death.

Victoria was at least on her guard. She stood there stiffly and tensely, not taking her eyes off Sissi. "Where is there supposed to be a body here?" she asked suspiciously.

"Down there." Sissi pointed behind her with her thumb. "She fell. No, I think she was pushed!"

She took a few more steps, but Victoria fortunately stayed where she was. "You said earlier that the dead woman was half buried in the ground..."

I breathed a sigh of relief because Victoria finally seemed to have realized that there was something very wrong with her companion and the story of her discovery of the corpse.

But Sissi suddenly stormed towards my poor human without any warning. A blade flashed in her hand, and she screamed: "You lousy little bitch, you'll never get your hands on my Leonard!"

I started to jump forward. *I can handle a knife*, I thought to myself. I'd had to take on worse weapons in the past.

I saw Sissi suddenly pull something out of her jacket pocket with her left hand. A black, cylindrical object—

which she pointed at me.

The next moment, a stinking cloud hit me right in the face. My eyes burned like fire! I was engulfed in pain and darkness.

I could no longer see anything. I landed, but not on the killer as I had intended. The leaves on the forest floor rustled under my paws. Victoria screamed.

Then I heard Pearl meowing in panic: "Athos, watch out, you're heading into the abyss!"

I had wanted to pounce again on the murderess right after I landed, but apparently she was no longer in the direction where I'd thought she was. And yet I smelled her?

Or was that just a memory? My snout was full of smoke; I couldn't perceive anything else, as I was no longer in control of my senses.

The world seemed to revolve around me, even though I could no longer see any of it. It felt like the ground was giving way beneath my paws. The pain traveled from my eyes to my entire head, and the acrid stench took my breath away.

"Pepper spray," Pearl commented. Then I heard her hiss. She probably wanted to throw herself at the attacker.

Victoria screamed, "No, Pearl!"

I heard Tiny land on the ground, roll a little, but then fortunately get back on her paws. She was now growling like a wild tiger.

But the two women's voices drowned her out. Both

were howling like two she-wolves going for each other's throats in a deadly duel.

"Pearl? What's the matter? Tell me what you see! You must be my eyes," I shouted.

I was struggling to stay on my feet, but I had to save Victoria. She was unarmed. She wouldn't be able to fend off this determined murderess for long.

And Pearl could not be allowed to attack again. In our duo, I was the one who was made to take hard blows—or stabbings. Even electric shocks if I had to. And now pepper spray! But any dose that harmed me could mean Pearl's end.

"Tiny?" I called out again. "You have to see for me! Which way do I have to jump?"

"Too dangerous! You could hurt Victoria," came the breathless reply.

Suddenly, a new smell hit my nose. Well, it wasn't really new—I knew it, but it was unexpected. The unmistakable scent of a lynx.

Moonshadow!

Only now did I hear him. The barely perceptible sound of his paws on the forest floor. His growl ... and then the scream of a woman. It was Sissi, not Victoria!

My heart almost stopped. All I could hear now was the sound of a powerful set of teeth smashing repeatedly into clothes, skin and muscles. Accompanied by Sissi's screams.

Then silence fell.

Moonshadow moved away as quickly as he had appeared. I heard a few more of his footsteps, then nothing more. His scent evaporated.

"Was that ... a lynx?" Victoria's voice came out rough and croaky.

The next moment, her breath hit me in the face. She suddenly knelt in front of me and wrapped her arms around my neck. "Athos? Are you okay? My poor, brave boy!"

I gave her a wet kiss. "I can't see anything. Am I going to be alright?"

It was Pearl—the crime expert—who answered my question, while at the same time hugging me and purring comfortingly. "In the movies, pepper spray usually doesn't last that long ... oh, wait, Victoria's reaching into the snow. You're about to get chilled."

My human put snow on my eyelids, which felt heavenly. But I had to sneeze violently a few times because the smelly pepper cloud was still burning my nose.

"What about Sissi?" I called out to Pearl.

"Moonshadow has done a great job," came the reply. "There's nothing more she can do to us."

"He killed her?"

"He did."

When I had attacked a murderer in the past, he had always escaped with his life. Somehow I had an inhibition about biting someone to death, even in self-defense.

But other laws prevailed in the wilderness. Any hesitation, any hint of compassion and the slightest squeamishness could mean your end. Eat or be eaten. Kill, or die yourself. Those were the rules here.

Moonshadow had not hesitated, and I couldn't say that I felt any great sorrow at the demise of a vile murderess.

35

After the police had finally finished questioning us, we managed to spend a few well-deserved days of vacation at the hotel together.

Victoria went cross-country skiing, Tim studied for his exam and Pearl and I didn't know what to do with all our free time at first.

Leonard Zauner invited us to be his guests at the Alpenrose for as long as we wanted. He was in shock, was being looked after by a police psychologist and found a lot of strength and support from his son, whom the terrible events had brought closer to him than ever before.

Tracy had a clarifying conversation with Victoria, during which she found out that our human had no interest in Alessio, even though he had shamelessly hit on her.

Tracy seemed relieved at first, but then burst into tears. "He just doesn't love me. I can do whatever I want, it's just never enough."

"You deserve better than that womanizer," said Victoria. "Someone who loves you for who you are without you having to bend over backwards for it. And that man, just right for you, is out there somewhere, I can promise you that. It may take a while to find him, but it will work out. In the meantime, just don't let guys like Alessio torment you."

She gently lifted the young barmaid's chin with two fingers and looked her in the eye.

Tracy sniffled. "You're right. I should never have listened to Sissi—her advice about men was full of poison. Just like herself." She suddenly stretched out her arms and threw them around Victoria's neck.

Of course, Pearl and I also contributed a few cuddles as a result. After all, we weren't just four-pawed detectives, we were also Victoria's co-therapists. And both Pearl and I were very proud of that.

In the afternoon of the same day, I took a nap on our patio. It had gotten warmer and the snow had melted, so Pearl joined me and took a siesta as well. That is, I thought she went to sleep too, but when I woke up later, I was alone.

I ran back into the room to Tim and Victoria, but found that Pearl wasn't with them. Fear immediately rose up inside me.

Tiny, where are you?

I ran back out onto the patio, where I pressed my nose against the flagstones and started sniffing. Pearl couldn't have flown away. I would find her.

Her trail led into the forest, even though I couldn't believe it at first. The fact that she had set off alone into the wilderness wasn't like her at all. I mean, she always claimed that she didn't need a canine bodyguard, but I wouldn't have thought she was that tired of living to walk out into the forest completely defenseless.

I ran faster. Fortunately, I had no trouble following her trail. Pearl's scent was as familiar to me as my own.

When I finally heard Pearl's voice, I breathed a sigh of relief. On the one hand that is—on the other hand, I didn't. I knew immediately whose company she was in.

Moonshadow.

It seemed to be a very personal and confidential conversation. The big lynx's voice sounded unusually gentle.

I stayed where I was and didn't make a sound, instead of covering the last bit of ground that would have led me to them. I was upwind of them, so not even Moonshadow's keen senses would register my presence.

"I have to leave here," the lynx said to Pearl in a serious voice. "Now that I've killed a human, I have to find a new territory. They will hunt me down."

"But only Victoria has seen you, and she's certainly not going to tell anyone," said Pearl. She sounded deeply despondent.

"I'm sure she has already told those people from the police who swarmed through my forest like flies, and they also could see my marks on the body. I overheard them; they were talking about me. That's why I have to get away from here, Pearl."

"And you waited to say goodbye to me?" she asked, touched.

The lynx's voice changed. Suddenly the big cat sounded years younger and rather uncertain.

"I was hoping ... well, I know this sounds crazy, but I wanted to offer you ... why don't you come with me, Pearl? I'd be delighted to have your company. You're equipped for a life in the wild, you do know that, right? Your fur is thick enough. You're brave and clever. And I would protect you from all dangers and make sure you always have plenty to eat."

But no salmon! I expected Pearl to object something like that.

But she didn't do that. She just said: "I know that. You'd take good care of me. And I'd certainly have a lot of fun with you. You're a wonderful cat."

"But...?" he asked.

"But I ... can't go with you."

"You don't want to give up your criminal cases?" he speculated.

"Yeah, that's right."

"And neither do you want to abandon your humans, I take it?"

"That's also true."

A brief silence ensued.

Then Pearl said: "You know, in truth, I could probably get by without any more murders. I mean, I'd miss the snooping, but I certainly wouldn't get bored by your side."

"Certainly not," Moonshadow confirmed.

"And my humans could do without me. They would

miss me, of course. But at some point they would just get a new cat. And that's a good thing."

"And yet you don't want to come with me?"

"I can't, because of Athos. He, um, needs me. I'm his ... pack."

"His pack? Surely he would rather have another dog than a cat as a pack mate, wouldn't he?" said the lynx. "A female dog, perhaps."

"Yes, hmmm. Of course. That is, no."

"No?"

Silence fell again.

I could barely hear Moonshadow's words when he spoke up again. His voice was much quieter. And even softer: "Could it be that it's not just Athos who needs you, Pearl? But you need him too?"

"A cat doesn't need a dog," protested the tiny one.

"Well, then maybe because you ... like him? Love him?"

"Love a dog? Me?" Pearl's voice was little more than a murmur now, too. She sounded surprised, but she no longer objected.

The lynx didn't say anything at first.

But then: "You're a remarkable cat, Pearl. I envy Athos. You and he must belong together."

And Pearl replied: "Yes, we do." Now there was no more confusion or astonishment in her voice.

The forest was completely silent, as if even the ancient fir and spruce trees were listening to the conversation between the two very different cats and holding their breath.

"Then it only remains for me to say goodbye to you, Pearl," I heard Moonshadow's velvety voice once again. "I wish you nothing but the best—and your friend too. Maybe we'll meet again one day, even if I don't know where I'll end up yet."

"I would be very happy about that," said the tiny one. "We'll keep our eyes open for you."

I stole away with silent steps. I hadn't felt this light since I was a puppy, and my heart leapt in my chest like a little bird.

36

As the end of our vacation approached, I expected that we would return to Vienna with Tim. He was keen to look for a new apartment, and Victoria had promised that she would help him. And she'd hinted that she wanted to spend a lot of time with him, too.

Perhaps on the way home we would take a detour to our original home in the Salzkammergut, which I hadn't seen for a while.

But things turned out differently for us once again.

The day before we were about to leave the Alpenrose, our friend from the North Sea island of Sylt, Chief Inspector Oskar Nüring, called.

Victoria and Tim took the video call together, on Victoria's laptop.

Pearl jumped excitedly into the picture to greet Oskar, and of course I also squeezed in between Tim and Victoria to say hello to the inspector.

"We really could have used you here!" I panted excitedly into the camera. And: "How are you coping without us on Sylt? Do you have to solve a lot of murders on your own?"

But the inspector hadn't called to talk about murders. He seemed very excited, almost as if he had won the lottery.

"Victoria, Tim, you won't believe what's happened!

Could you maybe meet me on January 31st? In Venice? I know that's just a few days away, but I'm a bit overwhelmed, I'm afraid..."

His voice almost overflowed with the report he now started to give us in breathless words. And his story was really quite crazy.

What Pearl and I were able to piece together was the following: Through a friend in Hamburg, he had met an extraordinary healer who had allegedly been able to cure people of their dementia in several documented cases. Which amounted to a medical miracle—actually impossible.

But Oskar still had hope that this lady might be able to help his wife, who was suffering from a very advanced stage of dementia and no longer even recognized her own husband.

"I was able to speak to the woman on the phone," the inspector reported, his cheeks glowing, "and although she is very busy, constantly traveling all over the world, she invited me—Marianne and me, that is, to Venice. She's staying with a family there that I also know, just for a few days. But she is confident that she can do something for Marianne. And that's why I absolutely have to go to Venice!"

"That sounds incredible," said Victoria. "I do so hope that she really can help your wife. But Tim and I ... I mean, we'd love to come and stand by you. But Tim has an exam at the university in Vienna."

"On February 1st, to be precise," said Tim, "and I'm

terribly behind in my studies. We had another murder case to solve here in Tyrol. Victoria almost lost her life."

The chief inspector's eyes grew wide. "Good heavens. You'll have to tell me all about it."

"You can go to Venice and meet Oskar and his wife," Tim said to Victoria. "And that miracle healer!"

"I would like to do that, but..."

She turned back to Oskar on the screen. "I don't quite understand how I can help you?"

The inspector grimaced. "I don't really believe in spiritual healers, Victoria. And I certainly don't want to fall for a fraud. I mean, the friend who drew my attention to the lady is also in the police force, and is certainly not a daydreamer. But still, it just sounds too good to be true."

He broke off and smiled sheepishly. "That's why I was hoping ... well, that you could take a closer look at this healer for me. That you would be there when she works with Marianne and give me your open and honest opinion. You are such a good judge of character and, as a psychologist, you have a completely different perspective to me. I want to do everything I can to save my wife, but I can't allow her to be even worse off afterwards than she is now."

"He needs our support and our knowledge of human nature," Pearl commented.

Victoria looked at Tim again. "You really wouldn't mind if I went to Venice with Oskar?"

"Of course not! Venice is great. Isn't Carnival coming

up soon?"

"It doesn't start until a few days afterwards," said the inspector. "But I think you can already see great masks and costumes in the city in advance."

I gave the screen a wet kiss. It would be wonderful to see our friend Oskar again. And I'd never been to Venice before.

"Finally a different kind of mission," I said to Pearl. "Not a murder case, but to investigate a spiritual healer. That sounds exciting!"

"Someone's bound to die," Pearl said dryly. "You can count on it! It's really nice of Oskar to keep providing us with new murder cases."

But this time, the self-proclaimed master detective was wrong in her assumption. Because our next corpse wasn't waiting for us in Venice, but would already fall before our paws on the journey there.

More from Alex Wagner

If you enjoy snooping around with Athos and Pearl, why not try my other mystery series, too?

Penny Küfer Investigates—cozy mysteries full of Old World charm.

Penny's murder cases take her to the most beautiful places in Europe and to popular holiday destinations around the world: from the Moselle to the North Sea, from the high Alps to the Caribbean, from Vienna to Paris and on the most luxurious cruise ships.
These fun and fast-paced mysteries will keep you turning the pages long into the night!

Murder in Antiquity—a historical mystery series from the Roman Empire.

Join shady Germanic merchant Thanar and his clever slave Layla in their backwater frontier town, and on their travels to see the greatest sights of the ancient world. Meet legionaries, gladiators, barbarians, druids and Christians—and the most ruthless killers in the Empire!

About the author

Alex Wagner lives near Vienna, Austria. From her writing chair she has a view of an old ruined castle, which helps her to dream up the most devious murder plots.

Alex writes murder mysteries set in the most beautiful locations in Europe and in popular holiday spots. If you love to read Agatha Christie and other authors from the Golden Age of mystery fiction, you will enjoy her stories.

www.alexwagner.at
www.facebook.com/AlexWagnerMysteryWriter

Copyright © 2024 Alexandra Wagner
Publisher: Alexandra Wagner

All rights reserved. This book or any portion thereof may not be reproduced or used in any manner whatsoever without the express written permission of the publisher, except for the use of brief quotations in a book review.
The characters in this book are entirely fictional. Any resemblance to actual persons living or dead is entirely coincidental.

Cover design: Estella Vukovic
Editor: Tarryn Thomas

Printed in Great Britain
by Amazon